He narrowed his eyes and looked at her a little more closely. 'Do we know each other?'

She shook her head, and the way the movement sent silky blonde hair swirling around her shoulders would have had him imagining his fingers winding through it had he not been ignoring that side of things in favour of finding out what this was all about.

'No,' she said. 'I mean, not really. At least not in the strictest sense of the word.'

'I'm afraid you've lost me.'

'It is all a bit bemusing, I'll grant you,' she said. 'But the thing is I've got myself into a bit of a fix and I need your help.'

'What kind of a fix?'

She blushed and shifted her weight from one foot to the other. 'I seem to have—ah—sort of invented a boyfriend.'

'Sort of?'

She sighed. 'OK, not sort of. I did invent a boyfriend.'

Dear Reader

Some people say that your schooldays, with few responsibilities, hordes of friends and long, long holidays, are the happiest of your life. Others add that, whether you loved them or hated them, they can shape you for years.

Who hasn't idly browsed through Facebook to see what's become of the class bully or the prettiest, most popular girl in the year? And who hasn't wished they could sail into a reunion looking a million dollars, brimming with confidence and showing everyone what a fabulous success of their life they've made?

That's perennially single Zoe Montgomery's plan when, against her better instincts, she decides to attend her fifteen-year school reunion. Her schooldays definitely *weren't* the happiest of her life, and much to her dismay they've subsequently had quite an impact, so she's out to get closure. But, as can happen with the best-laid plans, things rapidly go awry—and before she knows it she's not only invented a fabulous fake boyfriend, she's brought him to life. When gorgeous advertising exec and latest tabloid hottie Dan Forrester and a very active grapevine become involved things start to get *really* complicated!

The school reunion that I went to, which provided the initial spark for this story, wasn't nearly as dramatic as Zoe's, but I can't help wishing it had been! I had a blast writing Dan and Zoe's story—I hope you enjoy it.

Lucy x

THE REUNION LIE

BY
LUCY KING

First published in Great Britain 2013
by Mills & Boon, an imprint of Harlequin (UK) Limited.
Harlequin (UK) Limited, Eton House, 18-24 Paradise Road,
Richmond, Surrey TW9 1SR

© Lucy King 2013

ISBN: 978 0 263 23597 5

Harlequin (UK) policy is to use papers that are natural, renewable and recyclable products and made from wood grown in sustainable forests. The logging and manufacturing processes conform to the legal environmental regulations of the country of origin.

Lucy King spent her formative years lost in the world of Mills & Boon® romance when she really ought to have been paying attention to her teachers. Up against sparkling heroines, gorgeous heroes and the magic of falling in love, trigonometry and absolute ablatives didn't stand a chance.

But as she couldn't live in a dream world for ever she eventually acquired a degree in languages and an eclectic collection of jobs. A stroll to the River Thames one Saturday morning led her to her very own hero. The minute she laid eyes on the hunky rower getting out of a boat, clad only in Lycra and carrying a three-metre oar as if it was a toothpick, she knew she'd met the man she was going to marry. Luckily the rower thought the same.

She will always be grateful to whatever it was that made her stop dithering and actually sit down to type Chapter One, because dreaming up her own sparkling heroines and gorgeous heroes is pretty much her idea of the perfect job.

Originally a Londoner, Lucy now lives in Spain, where she spends much of the time reading, failing to finish cryptic crosswords, and trying to convince herself that lying on the beach really *is* the best way to work.

Visit her at www.lucykingbooks.com

To the class of 1990
(none of whom are anything like the girls in this story!)
and our fun and fabulous school reunion.

CHAPTER ONE

In all her thirty-two years, Zoe Montgomery had never once entertained a truly violent thought, but if one more person asked her whether she had a husband and children and then tutted in sympathy when she said she had neither she was going to have to hit something hard. Possibly the gin.

Did it matter that she'd been running her own mystery shopping agency for the past five years and was responsible for a two-million-pound turnover? No, it did not. Did anyone care that she'd started off refurbishing a tiny studio flat in an insalubrious part of London, sold it for double what she'd paid and had subsequently leapt up the property ladder to the spacious Hoxton maisonette she lived in now? Of course they didn't. And what about the doctorate she'd toiled over for five long but happy years? Did that have them gasping in awe? Not a bit of it.

All that mattered to the forty or so depressingly tunnel-visioned women gathered in the bar for their fifteen-year school reunion was that she was still single and childless.

Zoe gritted her teeth and knocked back a mouthful of lukewarm Chablis as the conversation about house prices, catchment areas and Tuscany rattled around the little group she'd been dragged into.

How she could ever have imagined her contemporaries would have changed was beyond her. Back in their board-

ing-school days, despite the best private girls' education
the country had to offer and despite a handful of intellects
far more formidable than her own, all most of them had
ever wanted to achieve in life was marriage to an aristo-
crat, an estate and a socking great bank balance, and judging by the number of double-barrelled surnames, titles and
diamonds being shown off tonight that had been accomplished with dazzling success.

Zoe sighed in despair. All that money spent. All that potential untapped. All that dedication and ambition so badly
mis-channelled. What a waste.

As this evening was turning out to be.

She'd been here for fifteen minutes, but it had taken
her only five to realise that there was little to no chance
of achieving any of the things she'd hoped to achieve by
coming.

When the email inviting her to the reunion had popped
up in her in-box a month ago her first instinct had been to
ignore it. While she appreciated the fantastic academic education she'd had and the sacrifices her parents had made
for her to have it, she'd never got on all that well with these
girls. She hadn't had anything in common with most of
them, and some of them—one in particular—had made
her life pretty miserable for the best part of seven years.
So without a moment's hesitation she'd replied that she was
busy, deleted the email and firmly put it from her mind.

She'd gone back to doing what she did best—work—
and buried herself in a whole load of statistical analysis for
one of her and her sister's biggest clients, and had been so
absorbed by the numbers and the implications they might
have that that should have been that.

But to her intense frustration that hadn't been that because despite its consignment to the bin the invitation
seemed to have opened up a Pandora's box of adolescent
angst, hormonal chaos, and brutal and painfully clear mem-

ories, and, as a result, over the past couple of weeks she'd found herself dwelling on her school days with annoying regularity.

It didn't matter how hard she tried to shore up her defences and push it all back, or how much she tried to concentrate on something else. Her memory hammered away, and beneath such relentless pressure the sky-high barriers she'd erected to protect her from those hideous years crumbled, leaving it to trip down lanes she'd blocked off long ago, picking at emotional scabs and prodding at the wounds beneath as it did so.

And once that had happened no amount of statistical analysis could stop her remembering the pain and suffering she'd endured.

The bullying had started off trivially enough. Books she'd needed for lessons had strangely disappeared, phone messages and letters hadn't been passed on and there'd been rumours that hinted at lesbian tendencies and had all twelve girls in her dormitory huddling into a group at the far end of the room, eyeing her with suspicion and whispering.

Then there'd been the snide remarks to her face, the ones that targeted her family, mocking her and her sister's need for scholarships and lamenting the fact that they didn't live in a draughty old pile in the middle of nowhere, didn't holiday in Barbados and Verbier, and had never been anywhere near Ascot, Glyndebourne or Henley.

At first Zoe had gritted her teeth and tried to ignore it, telling herself it would stop soon enough if she just knuckled down and got on with things. That they'd soon get bored and move on to easier prey.

But they hadn't got bored and it hadn't stopped, and her indifference had actually made things worse, escalating what had up to that point been bullying of the mental and emotional kind to the physical.

Sitting in front of her computer, her spreadsheet blurring in front of her eyes as the memories kept coming, Zoe had sworn she could still feel the tiny bruises from the sneaky pinches and the sharp pain from the surreptitious kicks she'd received on an almost daily basis. She'd thought she could still hear the snip of the scissors as one afternoon, while she'd been working head down at her desk concentrating so hard she'd been oblivious to anything else, they'd cut through the long shiny ponytail she'd had since she was six.

Mostly, though, she kept reliving the awful night following the one and only time she'd dared to retaliate, when she'd been pinned down and had had ouzo poured down her throat. She'd been found by the caretaker stumbling around the grounds at midnight, singing—badly—at the top of her voice, and taken straight to the headmistress, and as a result had been suspended a month before her A levels.

It had *not* been a good time, and even though she'd got over it all years ago the last thing she needed was an evening spent with fifty-odd reminders of what had definitely not been the happiest days of her life.

But then at some point during the last week or so, her previously rock-solid conviction that she was right not to attend the reunion had begun to wobble. The more she'd dwelled on what had happened, the more she'd begun to regret the fact that she'd done so little to stop it. OK, so it wasn't as if she were going home to her parents every evening and had been able to confide in them, but with hindsight she could have told *someone*.

Why she hadn't had started to bother her. What it said about her she wasn't sure she wanted to know. And as if the tendrils of doubt, self-recrimination and denial that were winding through her weren't enough, she'd begun to be hassled by an image of her sixteen-year-old self, standing there with her hands on her hips and pointing out that now would be the perfect opportunity to redress a balance that should have never been allowed to become so skewed in the first place.

Go and show them, the little voice inside her head had demanded with increasing insistence. *Go and show them how well you've done, that despite their best efforts to batter your confidence and destroy your self-belief they couldn't. Go and show them they didn't win.*

She'd tried to resist because she'd risen above what had happened long ago, she really had, and besides, she loathed conflict, hated having to make conversation and avoided social occasions like the plague and the combination of all three might well finish her off. But that little voice wouldn't shut up, and in the end she'd come to the conclusion that she owed it to her teenage self at the very least to try and make amends because, quite apart from anything else, if she didn't she wouldn't have a moment's peace.

So she'd emailed the girl organising the reunion to tell her she'd changed her mind, and that was why, fizzing with adrenalin, buzzing with fighting spirit and brimming with a confidence she rarely felt when confronted with the idea of people, she'd wriggled into a little black dress and heels and then trekked across the city to the gastro-pub in Chelsea on this late September Thursday night instead of spending the evening at home snuggling up to her laptop in her pyjamas as usual.

But if she'd known things weren't going to work out as she'd anticipated, if she'd known she was going to wind up drinking disgustingly warm wine while having to endure a whole load of 'do you remember when's and being made to feel inadequate, as if somehow she'd *failed* simply because she hadn't procreated, then she wouldn't have bothered.

Zoe drained what was left of the wine in her glass and set her jaw. She knew she hadn't failed. She'd achieved way more than many other women of her age and she was proud of the success she'd made of her life.

And so what if she wasn't married and didn't have children? And who cared if she had abysmal luck on the boyfriend front? She had a career she adored, supportive and loving parents and a great sister. While she wasn't averse to the odd date or two and possibly a relationship at some stage, she didn't *need* a man to complete her life, and she certainly wasn't sure she wanted the chaos and mess and general disruption that children caused.

No, she was perfectly content with the way things were and therefore she had no need to feel insignificant. No need to feel inferior or inadequate. No need to let herself be affected by the opinions of a bunch of women who shouldn't—no, *didn't*—matter.

And yet…

As the conversation drifted on around her, once again casually dismissing her achievements as of no consequence and instead turning to the stellar accomplishments of husbands and children, Zoe felt what was left of the adrenalin and confidence drain away, leaving a kind of desperate despair she hadn't experienced for fifteen years.

All she'd wanted to do tonight was exact retribution for everything she'd had to go through. All she'd wanted to do was impress the girls who'd tried so hard to stamp her out, stun them with her success and make them jealous of *her* for a change, but she hadn't even been able to do that. The only kind of success anyone here would be impressed by was the marital kind, and that she didn't have.

Retribution, it seemed, was no more within reach than it had been fifteen years ago. There was no redressing of any balance and there were no looks of envy being cast her way, and just like that she sank into deep despondency.

These women hadn't changed, and nor, it appeared, had she, because despite managing to convince herself otherwise, despite all her professional achievements and industry accolades and the self-assurance she'd gained through them, she still cared what a bunch of over-privileged and underachieving housewives thought of her. They still had the ability to demolish her self-esteem, which was pretty shaky at the best of times, with nothing more than the curl of a lip and the arch of an eyebrow, and they could still make a mockery of her confidence.

That she wasn't as over her school experiences as she'd so blithely assumed was a pretty devastating discovery and Zoe felt her chest tighten with something that felt a lot like panic as the questions began to ricochet around her head.

Why hadn't she changed? Why did it still matter what they thought? Would she ever not? Above all, was there *anything* she could do to fight back?

The talk turned to biological clocks, career women and what their lives must be lacking by being single—accompanied by several pointed looks in her direction. And whether it was a great tangle of fifteen-year-old emotion that was churning around inside her or the confusion or the panic at the thought that she wasn't nearly as in control as she'd envisaged she didn't know, but adrenalin was suddenly pounding through her once again. The blood was rushing in her ears and her heart was thundering, and unable to stop, unable even to *think* about what she was doing, she found herself raising her eyebrows and saying in a cool voice that didn't sound anything like hers, 'Who said anything about being single?'

CHAPTER TWO

IF HE'D KNOWN his usually fairly quiet and staid local pub was going to be taken over by a gaggle of expensively turned out but very loud and loquacious women Dan would have suggested somewhere else to meet Pete because the sickly combination of scents that filled the air was making his stomach churn, the noise level was making his head throb and none of it was conducive to a catch-up over a few drinks and a bite to eat with a friend he hadn't seen for months.

As it was, however, Pete had texted him to say he was running late and had then gone incommunicado, so unfortunately he didn't have any choice but to arm himself with a pint, find a table on the other side of the pub and if possible block out the racket and the toxicity of the air until Pete arrived and they could make their escape.

With that aim in mind, Dan shrugged off his jacket and pushed up the sleeves of his shirt and then, bracing himself, began to make his way to the far and marginally less crowded end of the bar.

He was so focused on his destination, so intent on ignoring the women and the noise that he didn't notice one of their party clap eyes on him and suddenly smile. Nor did he see her put down her drink, extricate herself from the melee and make a beeline for him.

In fact he didn't notice anything about her at all until

she was standing right in front of him, stopping him in his tracks and flashing him a dazzling smile, and then it was pretty impossible *not* to notice her.

Dan didn't have a chance to mutter an 'excuse me' and step to one side. He didn't have time to wonder why she was standing so close nor why her smile was so bright. He didn't even have a chance to check her out properly.

All he got was a fleeting impression of blonde hair, dark eyes and an overall sense of attractiveness before she flung her arms round his neck, plastered herself against him and gave him the kind of kiss that he'd have considered more appropriate if they were naked and in private.

But he couldn't think because on impact shock reeled through him, blowing his mind and obliterating almost every neuron he possessed. For a second it rendered him immobile too, but then his body dimly registered the fact that the woman arching herself against him was soft and warm and pliant, the hand on the back of his neck was singeing his skin like a brand and the mouth moving over his was hot and lush, and the whole bizarrely passionate package sent every one of his senses into overdrive.

For one crazy split second he wanted to whip his arms round her and pull her closer. He wanted to cave in to his instincts and the desire that was beginning to spark through him and open his mouth on hers so that they could kiss properly and he could find out what she tasted like.

With his surroundings disintegrating, his brain dissolving and his hands automatically moving to her waist, Dan was on the point of doing just that when something flashed in his peripheral vision. It seared through the haze in his head, lodged in his brain with the force of a blow dart, and he froze. The heat racing through him vanished as if doused with a bucket of iced water and desire evaporated, leaving him numb and stunned.

And then as the implications of that flash hit him his

brain cranked into gear and the stunned shock spiralled into appalled disbelief. What on earth was he doing? What was he *thinking*? Hadn't he learned *anything* from seeing the details of his last relationship splashed all over the front page of one of the country's smuttier tabloids?

With his blood chilling at the thought of just how reckless he'd almost been, Dan jerked back and pushed her away, barely able to believe he'd so nearly fallen for what *had* to be a ruse because who went round randomly hurling themselves at perfect strangers without *some* kind of ulterior motive?

He stared down at the woman standing in front of him, flicking a quick glance over her and feeling his stomach tighten at the sight of the body that had so recently been clamped against him, clad in a tight black dress that plunged at the front and stopped an inch above her knees. Below the hem her stockinged legs tapered down into the sexiest pair of black high heels he'd ever seen and he suddenly had a brutally clear vision of those heels sliding up and down his calves as he pressed her into his mattress and reacquainted himself with her body.

Which was not going to happen, he told himself darkly, snapping his gaze back up to hers and deploying the single-minded focus he was supposedly famed for. The way she looked was irrelevant. The way she'd felt pressed against him was irrelevant. What had just happened, on the other hand, wasn't, and he had to remember that.

'Who the hell are you,' he said grimly, 'and what do you think you're doing?'

Well, wasn't that the question of the century? thought Zoe, staring up at the man she'd spied, selected and then accosted, still buzzing from the feel of him as she'd thrown her arms around his neck and pressed her mouth to his. Truthfully she no longer recognised herself and she no longer had a clue what she was doing, which was rather disconcerting for someone who usually applied logic, reason and consideration to every aspect of her life.

While she could just about make excuses for fabricating a boyfriend for the purposes of getting even, embellishing the poor man's qualities until he'd sounded unbelievable even to her own ears had gone way beyond the boundaries of a good idea. And as for deciding to bring him to life, well, that had been downright insanity.

She briefly considered blaming the way that what had started out as a simple little lie had spun so ludicrously out of control on the gimlet she'd drunk, but that wouldn't be fair. Not when she'd only had one and she could usually get through three before feeling a bit on the wobbly side.

No. The truth of it was that the minute she'd mentioned her fictitious yet fabulous boyfriend she'd noticed the abrupt shift in attitude towards her, and as the attention had swung back to her she'd been swamped by a deluge of delight and triumph and above all relief that finally *something* had worked.

As her former classmates had naturally sought more information about this gorgeous/devoted/brilliant-yet-sensitive man, they'd asked increasingly tricky-to-dodge questions but she'd been so intoxicated by the gasps of envy and admiration at her answers and by the feeling of being accepted for once that she hadn't thought twice about the inadvisedly elaborate lies that she'd started to spin.

She hadn't worried she was getting in too deep, that she'd be tripped up. Why would she when she'd borrowed the story of her sister's whirlwind romance with her ex-husband? Their relationship might have ended in the divorce to end all divorces, but it had started out romantically enough, and Lily had shared details. At length.

The lies had tripped off Zoe's tongue with surprising ease, so much so that she'd found herself elevating him to practically fiancé status and hinting that he was on the point of proposing. This development *had* had her worrying that everything was getting a bit out of control, but her audience were so beside themselves at the news that she casually dismissed her concerns.

The admiration and envy that she'd been basking in were utterly shallow, of course, not to mention completely baseless, but it had felt *so* good to stand there as an equal for a change. To feel her rapidly dwindling self-esteem soar and everything else she'd been worrying about lately melt away. And to have them jealous of *her* for once. Particularly gratifying was the sucking-on-a-lemon look on the face of Samantha Newark, the newly installed Countess of Shipley and Zoe's number one tormentor, who might have swapped mousey frizzy hair and pie-crust collared blouses for a sleek blonde up-do and a designer wardrobe at some point in the last fifteen years, but was still, apparently, intent on being her bête noire.

So while inventing a boyfriend had been rash and mad and faintly pathetic, it had succeeded where her professional prowess had failed and Zoe had to admit that she couldn't entirely regret it.

She did, however, regret deciding to bring him to life, because for that there had been no excuse. She'd been doing marvellously, adeptly treading a fine line between awesomeness and implausibility and just about keeping on top of all the lies she was telling.

So what had happened? What had tipped her over the edge? When Samantha had scoffed at her and said he sounded far too good to be true, why hadn't she just shrugged nonchalantly and smiled enigmatically and left her to think what she liked? Why had she let it goad her into actually producing said boyfriend?

Had she got carried away by a false sense of security? Had she started to believe her own story? Or had it been wishful thinking that someone as fantastic as her fake boy-friend would actually turn up for real?

Whatever it had been, it had been a mistake, that much was certain. Because even as the words 'Oh, and here he is!' were spilling out of her mouth, a little voice inside her head had been yelling at her to stop, and the heady feeling of triumph had rapidly turned into alarm then panic and desperation and complete and utter disbelief that having come so far she was about to ruin everything.

Which she couldn't let happen, so what choice had she then had but to find a suitable candidate?

When she'd first spotted him she'd had no idea whether he was suitable. She hadn't even really clocked what he looked like; being a head taller than everyone else he was simply the first person she'd noticed. But then she'd registered the dark hair and the handsome face and, deciding he at least fulfilled the 'gorgeous' element of her fake boy-friend's qualities, she'd wasted no time in going after him.

The idea of kissing him, though, hadn't really come to her until she was standing in front of him, suddenly feeling warm and tingly all over. She'd somehow found herself staring at his mouth and she'd been filled with a quite desperate urge to know what it would feel like on hers.

Conveniently telling herself that, firstly, if he really had been her boyfriend kissing him would be a totally natural thing to do and that, secondly, even though he wasn't it would validate the fiction she'd created, Zoe had embraced the role, pressed herself against him and planted her mouth on his.

For the briefest of moments she'd got the impression that he'd wanted to kiss her back, but then he'd pushed her away. Which hadn't been the most auspicious of starts but perhaps one she would have anticipated had she not completely lost her marbles, because frankly if the roles had been reversed she'd have done the same thing.

However, right now hindsight and retrospective regret were pointless; having staked her claim on *him*, she could hardly go and find someone else. And with the evening teetering on the edge of a nail-biting climax she didn't want to leave.

So all she could do now was appeal to his better nature and put her case forward as best she could, and hope he'd take pity on her and agree to help her out.

'Well?' said Dan, thinking that whoever she was and whatever was going through her cunning little mind she'd had quite long enough to come up with a plausible story.

'My name's Zoe Montgomery,' she said, looking up at him and giving him a blinding smile that wasn't exactly a surprise seeing as she'd probably just made God knew how much money, 'but as for what I'm doing, well, that's something I've been asking myself quite a lot over the last half an hour.'

What did come as a surprise, though, he thought, narrowing his eyes and fixing her with a stare designed to discomfort and disconcert, was the way her smile seemed to slice through his suspicion and strike him right in the chest. It was undoubtedly down to the shock of the past five minutes still making a mess of his brain, but nevertheless it did prove that he needed to keep his wits about him, because right now he wasn't in the mood for smiles. Of any kind. 'Enlighten me,' he said abruptly.

At his tone her smile faded, much to his relief, and her eyes clouded over for a second. 'I'm not sure I can.'

'Well, try.'

'Look, you have every right to be furious,' she said with an apologetic shrug. 'I shouldn't have accosted you like that. I'm sorry.'

Dan gritted his teeth and ignored the sensuous way her

dress shifted over her body with the movement. 'If that picture ends up in the paper, you will be.'

She frowned. 'What?'

'The kiss,' he said flatly, ruthlessly stamping down the heat that threatened to shoot through him at the memory of how hot and soft she'd felt as she'd pressed herself up against him. 'The set-up.'

Her jaw dropped and what looked like genuine surprise flashed across her face. 'How could you possibly know about that? I only thought of it myself a minute or two ago.'

'Experience.'

Her eyebrows shot up. 'This has happened to you before?'

'Once.' And that was quite enough, he thought, snapping that train of thought off before it could take root and bring back all the feelings of foolishness, disillusionment and betrayal he'd experienced following his most recent ex-girlfriend's duplicity. 'And you might as well know now you won't get a penny. My lawyers will slap an injunction on you and your photographer friend so fast your head will spin.'

'What photographer friend?'

He glanced round in search of her camera-wielding pap sidekick, but whoever it was had clearly fled because from what he could see none of the people who surrounded them was showing the slightest bit of interest in either of them or the kiss that she'd just planted on him.

But that didn't mean he hadn't been there.

'Innocence doesn't suit someone who looks like a sexy fallen angel,' he said grimly, shifting his gaze back to her and watching her closely.

Her eyes darkened and her cheeks went pink while her lips parted to let out a little gasp. 'You think I look like a sexy fallen angel?' she echoed, her voice sounding a bit breathy.

With all that tumbling blonde hair, eyes the colour of liquid dark chocolate and those killer curves Dan actually thought she looked like every fantasy he'd ever had. To his consternation he could all too easily picture her lying sprawled on his bed, her hair fanning out over his pillows as he loomed over her, watching her writhe beneath him and listening to her pant and plead and beg him to do filthy things to her.

At the vividness of the image his head swam and the entire reason for this conversation nearly shot clean from his mind. Nearly, but not quite. 'With the morals of a phone-hacking tabloid journalist,' he added sharply, because it suddenly seemed important to remember that bit.

She recoiled and took a hasty step back. 'Crikey, that's a bit much, isn't it?' she murmured, staring at him in astonishment. 'It was only a quick kiss.'

Yeah, right, he thought, rather rattled by the discovery that the self-control he'd always taken for granted wasn't quite as rock solid as he'd assumed. 'And tell?'

'What?' She leaned in a little and regarded him closely, the astonishment making way for concern. 'Look, are you sure you're all right?'

No, he wasn't sure he was all right at all. He wasn't sure he'd been all right for months. Years, probably. But then maybe that was what happened when you'd been betrayed not once, but twice, by women you once trusted. Maybe it was perfectly natural to develop a cynicism that ran bone deep and a wariness that coloured practically every decision you ever made when it came to the opposite sex.

Dan shoved his hands through his hair and drew in a deep measured breath in an effort to regain some sort of grip on his control, because now he was coming down from the embarrassingly melodramatic way he'd reacted to the kiss she'd given him it was slowly beginning to occur to him that he might have got this wrong.

For one thing the woman who'd attacked him was look-ing at him with such an unusual combination of sincerity, concern and bewilderment, and, now he thought about it, an underlying hint of panic, that she'd have to be a better actress than he'd ever come across to portray such a con-vincing range of emotion. Her lack of guile seemed pretty genuine too, although given his track record perhaps he wasn't the best person to pass judgement on that particu-lar trait.

For another thing, if all she'd wanted was a picture of the kiss, having got what she was after wouldn't she now be making every effort to leave and go off in search of a buyer?

So maybe there was another reason she'd approached him, he thought, belatedly applying the logic he would have applied a while ago had she not stolen his brain. Maybe she made a habit of kissing random men. Maybe she'd taken one look at him and for some reason had been unable to stop herself. Maybe she was just mad...

Another flash caught his attention and he jerked his head away from the woman in front of him and scanned the room until his gaze fell on a guy holding a camera and taking a series of group shots of the women on the far side of the pub.

And then as he realised that the photos weren't of him, they weren't of her, and the guy with the camera wasn't a paparazzo, and that he *had* got it wrong, he inwardly groaned. God, maybe *he* was the one who'd gone mad.

'Forget it,' he muttered, briefly wondering whether at some point in the not too distant future he oughtn't address his attitude towards women because surely not *all* of them could be out for everything they could get.

'Not a chance,' she said with a little snort. 'Who *are* you?'

'Dan Forrester,' he replied and automatically braced

himself for the spark of recognition that usually came with his name.

But this time it didn't come. In fact, she was staring at him utterly blankly and he wasn't sure what to make of it.

'I don't mean to be rude,' she said, now looking a bit embarrassed, 'but is that supposed to mean something?'

'Doesn't it?'

She shook her head. 'I'm afraid not. But then I don't take much of an interest in anything other than work, so if you haven't appeared in *Significance* then it's entirely possible you've slipped beneath my radar.' She shrugged. 'Sorry.'

'Significance?'

'It's a magazine about statistics and data interpretation. Riveting if you're into that sort of thing, boring as hell if you're not.'

'And you are?'

She nodded. 'For my sins. I'm a statistician. But getting back to the point, I think you might have misinterpreted my kiss.'

No surprise there. Quite a shock though when her gaze dropped to his mouth and lingered for a second, and he found himself a split second away from grabbing her and kissing her in a way that left no room for misinterpretation.

Dan swallowed back the impulse, shoved his hands deep in the pockets of his jeans in case they got ideas and reminded himself to concentrate. 'So why did you throw yourself at me?' he asked, rather more interested in her answer than he thought he ought to be.

She snapped her gaze back up to meet his and gave herself a quick shake. 'Oh. Well. It was all part of my plan.'

'What plan?'

'The one I came up with five minutes ago.'

'That was quick.'

She sighed. 'Way too quick as it turns out. It's my very

makeshift, badly thought out, and with hindsight a total mistake plan.'

'But one that somehow involves me?'

'I was rather hoping so.'

'How?'

Her eyes clouded over again and the panic he thought he'd glimpsed earlier flared in their depths. 'I've got myself into a bit of a fix and I need your help.'

Her voice suddenly held a faint tremble and her body tensed and Dan went still, every instinct he possessed telling him to get away from her right now because, while he might have been wrong in his assessment of her motives earlier, he didn't do damsels in distress—however attracted to them he was—and he didn't do help, and nothing good would come of changing his mind about any of that now.

But although his brain was waving great warning signs alerting him to the possible dangers of sticking around, something was keeping his mouth from forming a parting shot and something was keeping his feet from moving. To his alarm he was rooted to the spot, strangely transfixed and unusually bothered by the desperation she was emanating, and he was mystified as to why. Surely he couldn't actually be *interested* in hearing her out, could he?

'What kind of a fix?' he muttered since he could hardly carry on standing there in silence.

'See that bunch of women over there?' She smiled over his shoulder at them and gave a little wave.

He winced as one of them shrieked with laughter. 'They're impossible to miss.'

'I know.'

'What's the occasion?'

'School reunion.'

'Fun?' He couldn't think of anything worse, but then he'd hated his school years.

She shuddered. 'Absolutely horrendous.'

'So what are you doing here?'

'I thought it would be cathartic.'

'And is it?'

'No.'

'Then why not just leave?'

'Another excellent question.' She sighed and bit her lip and his gaze dipped to watch, his mouth going dry as he involuntarily imagined nibbling on that lip himself. 'You'd think that would have been the sensible thing to do, wouldn't you? The *logical* thing... But tonight my common sense and logic seem to have deserted me.'

Dan cleared his throat and thought that the same could be applied to him. 'How unfortunate,' he said and told himself that it might be a good idea to try and stay cool and aloof if he was ever going to extricate himself from the mess he seemed intent on submerging himself in.

'It is. Very. It's never happened to me before.' She frowned. 'I don't normally go around kissing strange men, you know.'

'I'm glad to hear it.' And oddly enough he was. 'So why did you?'

She tilted her head and regarded him contemplatively, as if mentally debating whether and how to continue. 'Have you ever been to a school reunion hoping to impress everyone with the success you've achieved?' she asked eventually.

'No.' Hell would freeze over first. And besides, if anyone *was* interested they could read about it in the papers like everyone else seemed to want to.

'Well, I was.' She sighed. 'But it turns out that none of them could care less about any of that. All that any of them can bang on about is their husbands and children.'

At the resignation and disdain in her voice Dan couldn't help feeling a stab of sympathy despite his intention to remain detached, because he knew what it was like to be on the receiving end of that kind of conversation. 'Now that does sound bad.'

'It's *awful*. I have neither and there's only so much chat about school league tables and the importance of baby violin classes I can stomach, which is, I've discovered, not a lot.'

'I'm not surprised. How on earth does a baby get to grips with a violin?'

'I didn't dare ask.' She closed her eyes briefly, pinched the bridge of her nose and gave her head a shake of what looked like hopelessness. 'And they're the most appalling snobs.'

'Really?'

She nodded. 'I've never seen such one-upmanship and as for the name-dropping, well, if that were an Olympic sport there'd be golds all round.'

'Then why do you want to impress them?'

'It's a long and tedious story,' she said, before pulling her shoulders back and lifting her chin. 'Let's just say that I wasn't exactly the most popular girl at school and I ended up with the bruises to prove it.'

As the implications of that sank in Dan's jaw automatically tightened and his hands curled into fists because he knew about that too. His sister, Celia, had been bullied, and even though, unlike this woman, she'd eventually managed to deal with it, it was still a cause for regret that he'd been too busy dealing with the way he'd felt about their parents' divorce to realise what had been going on.

'I wanted retribution,' she added.

'I see,' he said, wishing not for the first time that he could string up every bully who'd ever existed and flog them to within an inch of their lives. 'So you were aiming for the living-well-being-the-best-revenge kind of thing?'

'Something like that.'

'Then what's the fix?'

She blushed and shifted her weight from one foot to the other and then took a deep breath. 'It didn't have the impact I was hoping for.' She stopped. Winced a little, he thought.

'And?' he prompted.

'And so I invented a boyfriend.'

His eyebrows shot up. 'What?'

She went red. 'Please don't make me say it again.'

'OK, but why?'

'Because I figured that that's the only thing they deem impressive.' She sighed. 'It's totally pathetic, I realise, but I seem to be sixteen all over again and, well, you know...' She tailed off and shrugged.

'Don't you have a real one?'

She flashed him a look of exasperation. 'If I did I wouldn't have had to invent one, would I?'

'I suppose not.' Although why she didn't when she looked like that and felt like that he had no idea.

'And I certainly wouldn't have been kissing you.'

Which would have been a shame, he thought, briefly distracted by the memory of her mouth moving against his. 'Did it work?'

'Like a dream. Or should I say a nightmare? Things have got a bit out of hand.'

'How?'

She shook her head as if utterly unable to comprehend what was going on. 'All I did was mention that I had a boyfriend, but I guess I should have realised they'd descend on that piece of information like a pack of starving hyenas. They started bombarding me with all these questions about what he did and where he was from, and things just kind of snowballed. They even started asking if he was The One.' She grimaced. 'I mean, seriously? Don't they know how statistically unlikely it is that you'll ever find The One?'

'Presumably not.'

'The chances have been calculated at around one in two-hundred-and-fifty-eight thousand, which I think you'll agree are not great odds.'

At her indignation, Dan felt his mouth twitch with the beginnings of a grin. 'They certainly don't sound that good.'

'They're atrocious, and the odds that there's only one One are even less. But anyway, I was in the middle of extolling my fictitious boyfriend's virtues, of which there are a *great* many, naturally—'

'Naturally.'

'When someone said a bit too sceptically for my liking that he sounded too good to be true and it wound me up. So I thought I'd collar the next vaguely presentable man who walked in and ask him to help. Then you showed up, and I thought *you'll do*.'

'Charming,' said Dan dryly, wondering whether he ought to be offended or impressed by her candour.

She shrugged. 'Sorry.'

Settling on the latter, he said, 'At least you're honest.' Which made a refreshing change when it came to the opposite sex.

'Hardly,' she said, giving him a wry smile. 'I've just spent every one of the last ten minutes lying my head off. I don't normally, but this evening I seem to have gone a bit off the rails. Hence the kiss,' she added, and then a look of horror crossed her face and her gaze dropped to his left hand as a thought evidently crossed her mind. 'God, you're not married or anything, are you?'

'No.' Much to his mother's continual and extremely vocal disappointment.

'Girlfriend?'

'Not at the moment,' he said, just about managing to hold back the shudder that wanted to run through him at the thought.

She gave him a bright smile and let out a long breath. 'Oh, that *is* a relief.'

'Isn't it?' And not just for her. 'Although if I'd had either I'm not sure they'd have been all that impressed at what just happened.'

'No,' she conceded. 'But then you could always have told them I started it.'

He tilted his head and shot her a sceptical look. 'Would *you* settle for that?'

She stared at him in surprise. 'Why not? It's the truth, isn't it?'

'When does that ever matter?'

'You sound cynical.'

'Just being realistic.'

'Maybe you should get some new friends.'

'Maybe I should.'

'Anyway,' she said, 'if I trusted you, of course I'd believe you.'

She made it sound so simple. 'Then you're unlike virtually every woman I've ever met.'

Her smile faded. 'I expect I am,' she said with a resigned sigh.

'Which is not necessarily a bad thing.'

'If you say so,' she muttered, sounding so thoroughly unconvinced and down that he had an unexpected urge to haul her back into his arms and tell her everything was going to be all right.

Failing to understand what was going on with that, Dan parked it and pulled himself together. 'What would you have done if I *had* had a wife or girlfriend?'

'I'm not sure,' she said, thinking about it for a moment. 'Slapped you to make it look like an argument and stormed out probably.'

He winced. 'Ouch.'

'Quite. So it's lucky for both of us you don't, isn't it?'

She took a step towards him and looked up at him beseech-
ingly, and as her scent wound through him his head briefly
swam. 'So what do you think?' she asked softly. 'Will you
help me out and play the part of my besotted boyfriend for
a bit or do I need to slink out and hope I don't see any of
that lot ever again?'

CHAPTER THREE

ABSOLUTELY NO WAY was the answer that was hovering on the tip of Dan's tongue as he looked down at Zoe and steeled himself to ignore the shimmering hope in her eyes. She might not be the kiss-and-tell girl he'd initially suspected her of being—and the story she'd subsequently spun him was too convoluted to be anything but the truth—but going along with her ridiculous proposition was still out of the question.

Even if he had possessed a chivalrous streak—which he most certainly didn't—ever since he'd shot to the top of that bloody eligible bachelor list five years ago he'd had the press nosing around his private life, commenting on his relationships and speculating about whether he had any intention of settling down. And following the hideously detailed story Jasmine had sold six months ago, he now hit the headlines pretty much every time he even *spoke* to a woman, and he had no desire to fan the embers with yet more fodder for gossip.

God only knew how far this particular little farce had gone, but should it get out that he was romantically involved—falsely or not—there'd be repercussions he could barely bear thinking about.

And not just from the press.

Ever since he'd turned thirty his mother had never passed up an opportunity to mention how she wasn't getting any younger and how she'd like to be able to enjoy her grandchildren while she still could, and, although he hadn't reached *his* breaking point yet, the memories she stirred up every time she mentioned it were getting harder and harder to suppress and he wasn't sure how much longer he could stand it.

If *she* got to hear of a relationship then his life would become truly intolerable, so if he had any sense whatsoever he'd be saying goodbye and good luck and sticking to his original plan of buying a pint and taking himself off to a relatively quiet corner of the pub. Even more wisely he'd be heading out of the pub altogether, finding a venue that didn't contain lunatic women with hyperactive imaginations and texting Pete to inform him of the change of plan.

But Zoe had clearly stolen every drop of sense he possessed because she was blinking up at him with those pleading brown eyes fringed with the thickest darkest eyelashes he'd ever seen, and all he could think about was how she'd felt plastered up against him, how warm and soft she'd been and how desperate she was looking now.

He didn't think he'd ever seen quite such raw panic or such heartfelt pleading before, and it was making his resolve not to get involved waver. It was giving rise to a weird protective streak that he hadn't known he'd had and an oddly difficult to ignore sense of empathy.

Even though he'd always considered himself to be way too canny and too cynical to be suckered by a damsel in distress, he did know what it was like to be bombarded with the whole marriage and children thing so relentlessly that you could be driven to recklessness. He did know what it was like to go off the rails and make rash decisions that with hindsight were just plain madness.

So if he could figure out something that wouldn't require much input from him but would have the maximum impact for her, if it was only for a moment and strictly on his terms, then maybe, just maybe, he *could* help her out.

Zoe bit her lip nervously, as if trying to stop herself from telling him to hurry up, and as his gaze dipped to her mouth the solution came to him in a flash.

'All right,' he said, dismissing the voice in his head demanding to know whether he truly had gone insane, because, really, what harm could come of it? 'You can have a kiss.'

Oh, thank God for that, thought Zoe letting out the breath she hadn't realised she'd been holding.

For one horrible moment she'd thought Dan was going to say 'no' to her frankly preposterous proposal, declare she was mad and march off. Like any normal person—as unlike her he seemed to be—would. But he hadn't. Her decision to enhance her appeal to his better nature with a whole load of very uncharacteristic eyelash batting had worked and he'd capitulated.

Well, sort of, she amended. A kiss wasn't exactly what she'd been hoping him to offer, but it was a start.

'Haven't I already had one of those?' she asked.

His eyes glittered as he considered. 'I'll make it a proper one. In full view of everyone. To make up for any doubts that might have been generated by my pushing you away the last time.'

'I see,' she said, having to concede that this was a good idea. 'And then what?'

'I'll be leaving.'

'Oh.' Zoe felt her face begin to fall and pulled herself together. What had she been expecting? That he'd want to stick around and get even more involved in the craziness she'd created? Why on earth would he—or anyone for that matter—want to do that? She ought to be grateful that he'd offered a kiss, not left her to face the repercussions of her little white lies.

'Think of it like this,' said Dan. 'I popped in to say hello on my way to somewhere else, and once we've had the kiss I'll be popping out again. You can do what you like.'

Logically Zoe knew that that was fair enough, but the thought of all those women eagerly waiting to meet him and the giddy rapture that would ensue when they did was still battering away in her head and scrambling her powers of reason. 'Are you sure you wouldn't like to stay?'

'I don't think that's a very good idea, do you?'

Well, yes, actually she did, because if she was being brutally honest she didn't want to say goodbye to him just yet. She wasn't sure why, but she wanted more of him. 'Why not?'

He frowned. 'How deep are you in with the details, Zoe?'

She sighed. 'Pretty deep, I guess.' Not quite in over her head, but nearly. 'I think I might have implied that you're on the point of proposing.'

She thought she saw him shudder, which kind of told her what he thought of *that* particular idea.

'Then you should be counting yourself lucky you've got away with it this far,' he said. 'If you add me into the mix any further when I don't have any idea of the lies you've been drumming up things could get really complicated, don't you think?'

Hmm, he did have a point. 'Probably,' she muttered.

'Definitely,' he said, his dark eyes glittering in the soft light of the pub. 'So that's the deal, Zoe. One kiss. Take it or leave it.'

Well, what option did she have under the circumstances but to agree? she thought, caving into the common sense she usually valued so highly but seemed to have abandoned tonight.

Dan was absolutely right, of course. There was no probably about it. She'd pushed her luck way beyond its limit
this evening and sailed so close to the wind with the story
she'd concocted, and what with the emotional turbulence,
the stress of having to think on her feet and the horrible
sensation that her control was history she didn't think her
nervous system could take any more.

To carry on with the charade would be beyond reckless.
She could see that now. She'd achieved what she'd set out to
do and she'd got at least *some* sort of closure to her school
days, so there was no need to continue with it any longer.

Therefore Dan wouldn't be the only one leaving once
this kiss was over and done with. She'd be right with him.
Hanging off his arm, flinging a wave in the direction of
her former classmates and sailing out. Quitting while she
was still ahead. Leaving with her head held high and her
self-esteem not quite as close to rock bottom as it had been
before. And then she'd be heading for home, putting the
whole crazy night behind her and moving on.

It had better be one hell of a kiss, though. Her commitment to the idea was irrefutable. Just the thought of having
his mouth on hers, properly this time, was making her heart
thump and her knees wobble. His, on the other hand…Who
knew how he was intending to approach it?

'OK, well, fine,' she said, feeling all hot and tingly again
at the prospect of the two of them kissing, 'but could you
at least try and make it look convincing?'

Taking her hand and tugging her towards a gap in the
crowds from where they'd have maximum exposure, Dan
shot her a quick smouldering smile. 'I'll do my best.'

In the event, Dan didn't have to try all that hard to do his
best. Zoe's instant, scorchingly hot response to him—the
way she melted into him with a soft sigh, the tightening
of her arms around his neck and the pressure of her pelvis

tilting up against his, and then the little moans she started making at the back of her throat—was as mind-blowing as his was to her, and within seconds the kiss had taken on a life of its own.

Kissing a woman certainly wasn't something he'd never done before. On the contrary it was an activity he'd engaged in a lot during his thirty-three years, generally with great success, but he'd never had a kiss quite like this one. He'd never had his mind go quite so blank quite so fast. He'd never had the feeling that the world around him was disintegrating. And he'd never experienced such a swift rush of desire, such instant heat nor such a reckless longing to toss aside his control and give in to such clamouring raw need.

Who knew where the intensity of it, the insanely desperate urge to flatten Zoe against the nearest suitable surface and get her naked, came from? It could have simply been down to intense and sizzling chemistry that now surged between them. It could have merely been that emotions seemed to be running fever high this evening. Or it could have been the fact that the three-date-only rule he'd instigated following Jasmine's blabbing to the press usually precluded sex by its very nature, and he was missing it. Whatever it was, and, really, his brain was in no state to try and work it out, Dan didn't want the kiss to end.

And it might not have done had a distant wolf whistle followed by a cut-glass-accented suggestion they get a room not sliced through the fog in his head and brought him thumping down to earth.

Reluctantly drawing back, he stared down at the woman in his arms. Her eyes were glazed, her cheeks were pink and her lips were rosy from the pressure of the kiss, and her breathing was all ragged and shallow. She looked as shaken as he felt and at the realisation that she'd been as affected as he had his self-control rocked for a second. He could still feel every inch of her pressed up against him, was achingly aware of her breasts crushed to his chest and all he could think about was doing it again.

But he couldn't do it again, could he, because one kiss had been the deal and that had been accomplished. More thoroughly and disturbingly than he could ever have imagined.

'Thanks,' said Zoe huskily, unwinding her arms from around his neck and placing her hands on his chest instead.

'You're welcome.'

She tilted her head and a slow sexy smile curved her mouth. 'That should have done it, don't you think?'

'Done what?' he muttered, too dazzled by the smile and too preoccupied and baffled by the way his skin was burning beneath her palms and his blood was still burning through his veins to have a clue what she was talking about.

'Convinced them.'

For a moment he was about to ask 'They who?' but he managed to pull himself up just in time as his brain cleared enough for reason to put in an appearance. Right. Her ex-classmates. The bullies. The reason for the kiss. 'If it didn't I can't imagine what would,' he muttered.

Her gaze dropped to his mouth and her eyes darkened, and the expression on her face suggested she was tempted to suggest another one. But she didn't, thank God, or heaven only knew what he would have done.

'So now I suppose you'll be off,' she murmured, lifting her eyes to meet his once again.

He nodded. 'I will.'

She tilted her head. 'Pity. In a way.'

Yes, it was, he thought, momentarily distracted by the intensely fiery look of desire in her eyes and the reciprocal surge that shot through him. And didn't that pull him up short, because his agreement to help Zoe out had been conditional on his participation being brief and on his terms, and the thought that he could so easily be persuaded into something more was deeply unsettling. 'But necessary. In another.'

'Then you'd better let me go.'

'Right.' He had. So why were his arms tightening around her instead of loosening? Why wasn't he turning on his heel and getting out of there just as fast as was humanly possible?

Oh God, he thought, his heart thudding with alarm and his entire body going still. What the hell was going on? Surely he wasn't thinking of staying, was he? He couldn't. He'd be nuts to even consider it.

So why was he now wondering if he could do more to help Zoe, the way he should have helped Celia? Why was a flicker of the guilt that he thought he'd dealt with years ago now leaping around in his stomach and battling with desire?

He couldn't stay, he reminded himself firmly, setting his jaw and ruthlessly stamping out the guilt. He didn't need to. Celia was fine. She hadn't needed him. The two cases bore no resemblance whatsoever. Besides, the potential fallout from being some kind of white knight here was huge, and why he kept forgetting that he had no idea.

Or was it as big a deal as he was making out?

Zoe hadn't recognised him, he realised, his head suddenly pounding with possibilities. No one else here seemed to. Had he really become so paranoid that he thought everyone everywhere was out to get him? Was he really so vain that he thought everyone knew who he was? And how long was he going to let what Jasmine had done influence his decisions?

'Dan?'

The sharpness of Zoe's voice jerked him out of the tangled confusion of ideas and thoughts churning around his head. 'What?'

She pushed at his chest. 'Let me go.'

'In a minute.'

'What?' Her eyes widened and filled with alarm that mirrored his own. 'No. Now.'

'Why?'

'*Why?* Because it's what we agreed, and if you don't release me right now it'll be too late.'

It already was. At least for him. Because now all he could think was that he could help her. That he had to help her. 'What if I've changed my mind?'

She looked aghast. 'You can't.'

'Why not? I got the impression you wanted more from me than just a kiss.'

'Maybe, but that was before.'

'Before what?'

'Before I changed my mind too. You were absolutely right. I'm in way too deep for this kind of thing. I've had enough and I really don't think I can take any more.' She flicked a quick glance to her right. 'Oh, God, they're on their way over, and believe me you do not want "us" to be subjected to the horror that is Samantha Newark.'

Dan felt a shudder rip through her and any lingering doubt that he was doing the right thing instantly vanished. 'Is she the one who gave you the bruises?'

She looked back at him as confusion flickered across her face. 'What? Oh. Well, yes, but who cares about that now? If we don't leave right this minute, as you so cleverly pointed out things will get really complicated.'

He set his jaw. 'Complication is my middle name.'

'What?' she asked with something akin to panic. 'No. This is insane.'

'You started it,' he felt obliged to point out.

'And I want to finish it.'

'So let's finish it. Properly.'

'I'm trying to,' she said through gritted teeth.

'Where's your spirit of adventure?'

'I don't have one.'

'I find that hard to believe. Haven't you just produced a boyfriend out of thin air?'

'Would you mind keeping your voice down?' she said in a furious low voice.

'And that kiss was something else.'

'Forget the kiss,' she practically hissed.

'I don't think that's going to be possible.'

'It has to be.'

He pulled her close and looked deep into her eyes. 'You know, we should do this. *You* should do this.'

'In the name of all that's holy, why?'

'My sister was bullied and it was only when she stood up to them that she got over it. You need to deal with it so you can move on.'

'I have, thank you very much, Mr Amateur Psychologist, and I am.'

He arched a sceptical eyebrow. 'Really?'

'OK, so I'm a work in progress.'

'I can help.'

'They'd see through us in a second.'

'No, they wouldn't. I'm in advertising.'

For a second she just stared at him in uncomprehending disbelief. 'What on earth does that have to do with anything?'

'It involves manipulating perception and getting people to believe what they're told regardless of whether it's the truth or not, and I'm an expert.'

'Your cynicism runs deep.'

'Luckily so does my creativity.'

'Believe me, it's not a patch on mine,' said Zoe darkly. 'You do *not* want to hear the stuff I've made up.'

'Don't I? I'm rather keen to find out the exceptional talents you've given me.'

She clutched at his shirt and stared at him wildly. 'Why are you being so persistent about this?'

'I don't think I want to let you go just yet.' Of everything
that had been running through his brain that was the one
thing of which he was certain. He wanted some more of
those kisses. He wanted more of her.

'So let's talk on the pavement outside. Let's go to a different bar, a restaurant, anywhere away from here.'

'I also don't like bullies.'

'Neither do I, but they're mine to deal with, and—'

'Zoe!'

'Oh, God,' she muttered, her voice shaking as the stri-
dent female tone came from right behind them. 'I *told* you
it would be too late.' She dropped her head onto his chest.
'This is going to be a disaster,' she said, her words muffled
against his shirt. 'A total unmitigated disaster.'

Despite Zoe's misgivings, her frustration that her escape
plan had been thwarted and her deeply felt conviction that
Dan had ruined everything, things weren't turning out to
be as bad as she'd anticipated.

With her contemporaries flocking around them she really had feared the worst, but by that stage she'd had no
choice but to extricate herself from Dan's arms to face Samantha and her little bunch of cohorts and imminent disaster.

Lacking his confidence, she'd made the introductions
with apprehension and nerves twisting her stomach into
knots, absolutely certain that the women, Samantha especially, would immediately see straight through her, Dan
and their pseudo romance. She'd been waiting on tenter-
hooks for the fragile house of cards she'd built to collapse,
and preparing herself to run and hide and never show her
face in public again.

But in fact things couldn't be going better, and she was
beginning to think she actually ought to be thanking him
for making her follow through with this.

Once the introductions were out of the way and drinks had been bought Dan had slid into the role of her boyfriend with surprising ease, swapping small talk with aplomb while displaying such an impressively wide knowledge of everything from London's social calendar to Tuscan hot spots that she didn't think he was even having to fake it.

He certainly couldn't be faking the charm with which he had people eating out of his hand. It was totally natural, dazzling and hypnotic, and she could only envy the way he was entertaining everyone so effortlessly and so compellingly that they were buzzing round him like social climbers in the vicinity of a member of royalty.

OK, so it probably didn't hurt that he was so gorgeous to look at, she had to admit, casting a surreptitious glance up at him over the rim of her glass. She felt the oddly drugging heat that had filled her when they'd kissed properly begin to spread through her again, but it was more than that. It was something within him, something powerful, magnetic and totally mesmerising, and it made the Dan she'd first met seem nothing more than a brief aberration.

If she weren't so distracted by the aftermath of that kiss and the weird swimming sensation going on in her head she'd be watching and learning, because while she sucked at interpersonal relationships she had the impression that Dan Forrester excelled at them.

'So, Dan,' she heard Harriet née Williams now Denham-Davis and one of Samantha's more docile cronies say. 'Zoe tells us you're *hugely* successful.'

Tuning back into the conversation she should never really have left, Zoe fought the urge to roll her eyes and gazed up at him with what she hoped was adoration instead.

'Oh, I don't know about that,' he said, smiling down at her so warmly that her insides went all fluttery. 'She over-exaggerates, don't you, darling?'

'I couldn't possibly, Honeybun,' she said, flashing him

a dazzling smile in return and marvelling at the way he
didn't even bat an eyelid at the cringe-worthy term of en-
dearment she'd given the girls when she'd been asked what
her fictitious boyfriend was called and had been unable to
drum up a suitable name fast enough.

'What field are you in?' asked Harriet.

'Advertising.'

'Ooh, how dashingly creative,' she said. 'Which firm?'

'DBF Associates.'

Crikey, thought Zoe with a bit of a start. Even she'd
heard of that one. It was one of the most successful advertising agencies in London. She'd read somewhere that it
was cutting-edge and award-winning and employed only
the best.

'And what do you do there?' asked Harriet.

'I own it.'

Zoe just about managed to keep her jaw from hitting the
floor, because for one thing what Dan did for a living—
and she couldn't see why he'd be making this up when he
hadn't had to make anything up so far—was surely something his adoring girlfriend would know, and for another
what was so surprising about the fact that he ran his own
successful business? After all, *she* did, didn't she, and she
was a lot less sorted than he seemed to be.

Still, she couldn't help being impressed—although perhaps not in the same way as Harriet and Samantha, who
were letting out little sighs of approval while the pound
signs, she fancied, lit up their eyes and the sounds of *ker-
ching* rattled through their brains.

'And would you be one of the Ashwicke Forresters?'
said Harriet, having established Dan's professional and,
by extension, financial status and clearly deciding to move
on to the social.

'I am,' he said.

Who or what the Ashwicke Forresters were remained a

mystery to Zoe, but Harriet was practically quivering with delight—even the navy velvet Alice band that Zoe suspected was the same one she'd worn at school trembled—and her eyes were sparkling. 'Oh, how thrilling. I met your parents once years ago. At the Queen Mary's Ball, I think it was. Absolutely delightful. How *are* they?'

'Divorced,' he said flatly.

'Oh,' said Harriet, her eyes widening and losing some of that sparkle as the air thickened with awkwardness. 'Well. I'm sorry to hear that.'

'Are you?' Dan said archly, and as Zoe caught a trace of steel beneath the charming exterior she felt her heartstrings twang. Clearly the subject of his parents' divorce was a touchy one. As was marriage perhaps, she thought, because gorgeous successful single men over the age of thirty who didn't have a problem with commitment or excess emotional baggage were rare. So should the conversation ever get round to the imminent proposal she'd hinted at—and in all honesty she didn't hold out much hope that it wouldn't—maybe she could do him a favour and release him from that particular obligation.

His abrupt tone might have tugged at Zoe's heartstrings, but it had taken the other two very aback if the lull in conversation was anything to go by. However, St Catherine's girls never let conversation stagnate for long, and Zoe wasn't the least bit surprised to see Samantha recover first.

'Oh, I recognise you now,' she said with a gleam in her eye and a faintly triumphant smile on her lips, neither of which Zoe liked the look of at all. 'You're *that* Dan Forrester, aren't you?'

CHAPTER FOUR

IF EVER THERE was a moment to be off this was it, thought Dan darkly as this bombshell once again rendered their little group momentarily silent, because in his blithe assumption that he wouldn't be recognised he'd clearly been a naïve idiot. He wasn't vain and he wasn't arrogant but he *was* a bloody fool, because he could virtually see ears pricking and antennae quivering, he could practically hear the grapevine beginning to tremble, and it struck him that there was now *every* chance that this little charade would eventually end up in the news.

As a result he was in something of a quandary. If he stayed he'd undoubtedly be digging the hole he was in deeper, but if he left he'd potentially be adding another dimension to the story, because now he thought about it his departure could well be construed as him giving a damn about what Jasmine had done. Which he didn't. At least not much.

So what should he do?

For a split second he hesitated while swiftly weighing up the pros and cons of each option, and then he made his decision. If he left, the outcome of the evening would be out of his hands, it could well end up in the press anyway and the likelihood was that his pride would end up dented all over again. But if he stayed, well, at least he'd be able to exert some sort of control over the proceedings.

Besides, the hole he was in was entirely of his making. Zoe had tried to dissuade him from the course of action he'd decided to follow but he'd been absolutely hell-bent on it, thick-headedly bulldozing through every one of her very valid objections, so if he really had the integrity he thought he did he owed it to her to see it right through to the end, wherever and whenever that might be.

He might even find it fun in a crazy kind of way, he thought, deciding he might as well try and put a positive spin on it. He'd been heading up his own company for the best part of six years, gradually handing over more of the creative work to his colleagues so he could concentrate on the business and management side of things and he'd been missing it.

So he'd go with the flow. Listen and watch carefully and respond accordingly. He'd follow Zoe's lead, maybe set up a few of his own. Give it the one hundred per cent dedication he gave everything he did.

Aware that everyone was, at the moment, watching *him*, Dan squared his shoulders, looked Samantha straight in the eye and said, 'I suspect I am.'

Zoe squeezed his arm in a gesture he presumed was meant to be reassuring but wasn't, although what with the way it pressed her breast against his bicep it did give him the idea of keeping her close. 'His fame precedes him,' she said, with a mixture of misplaced enthusiasm and pride.

'It certainly does,' murmured Samantha, the hard glint in her eye and the air of bitchiness enveloping her reminding him that she was the sort of woman he couldn't stand and certainly would never trust, even if he *had* had the ability to do so. '*How* long did you say the two of you had been going out, Zoe?' she asked.

'Six months,' said Zoe dreamily, still clinging onto him and making his head swim a little with her proximity as he slid an arm around her waist and settled his hand on her hip. 'Six long happy months.'

Despite the heat rushing along his veins as her warmth and her scent wound their way through him Dan couldn't help shuddering because, God, real or not, six months now sounded absolutely terminal.

'But six months ago weren't you dating Jasmine Thomas, Dan?' said Samantha silkily, and he felt Zoe stiffen at his side, although whether in response to his shudder, the thought he might have been two-timing her, or the fact that presumably she hadn't prepared for this he had no idea.

'I was,' he said since there was no point in denying it.

'Who's Jasmine Thomas?'

'An actress,' supplied Harriet.

Having clearly spent a lot of the evening thinking on her feet, Zoe arched an eyebrow in an excellent portrayal of an indignant girlfriend, looked up at him accusingly and said, 'You never told me about her.'

'No, well, it's not something I choose to dwell on,' Dan said, wondering if the discomfort he felt whenever he was reminded of it would ever ease.

Samantha, on the other hand, he thought, catching a tiny flare of triumph in her eyes, looked about as comfortable as it was possible to be because she was clearly in her absolute element here. 'She sold her story about your relationship to the press, didn't she?'

'She did.'

'God, how *awful*,' said Zoe, pity and sympathy written all over her lovely face and shimmering in her mesmerising eyes as she gazed up at him. 'Why did she do it?'

'I broke up with her.' The minute a flowery wash bag had unexpectedly appeared in his bathroom a month after they'd started seeing each other and she'd stormed out accusing him of being a cold, aloof commitment-phobe.

'So it was a spurned lover kind of thing?'

'I guess.'

Zoe sniffed. 'What a cliché.'

It wasn't just a cliché, he thought darkly. It was also a pain, and frankly he was utterly fed up with the way that what Jasmine had done continued to linger. It had been six months ago, for heaven's sake, yet it showed no sign of being today's fish and chip wrapping. All he wanted was to forget about it, but he wasn't being allowed to.

'Didn't you know?' asked Samantha, snapping her focus round to Zoe.

'Oh, well, we've been rather wrapped up in our own little cocoon of love, haven't we, Honeybun?' Zoe murmured, sliding her hand to his lower back and beaming up at him soppily.

'We have.' He dropped a quick hard kiss on her cheek and felt her shiver.

'You've certainly managed to keep it extremely quiet,' said Harriet.

'Are you surprised?' said Dan.

'And what about all those other women?' asked Samantha.

Zoe lifted her eyebrows a millimetre or two. Other women? she mouthed.

'Smokescreens,' said Dan.

'So were you still dating this Jasmine woman when we met on that ski-slope in the Italian Alps?' she asked, with a look that suggested he'd better have been telling the truth about his creative skills.

'Of course not,' he said, rising to the challenge with the glimmer of a smile. 'We broke up a good fortnight before I spied you in your skin-tight black ski-suit.'

'My skin-tight black ski-suit?' She frowned. 'I thought you'd been as impressed by my mastery of the black runs as I'd been by your skill on the mogul field.'

'Nope,' he said. 'It was definitely the sexy ski-suit.'

'So it was the way I looked that made you ask me out to the nightclub that night?' she asked, smoothly steering him back on track.

'It was.'

Zoe tutted. 'So shallow.'

'Well, what can I say? You zoomed past me too fast for conversation. I just thought you were hot.' He ran his gaze over her and felt the heat whip through him. 'I still do.'

Her eyes darkened and she pressed a little closer and, his mouth suddenly dry, Dan lifted his pint to his lips and swallowed back a couple of large, much-needed gulps.

'The feeling is, and was, mutual,' she said a little huskily. 'Obviously. Otherwise I'd never have gone to bed with you on our first date.'

Dan nearly choked on his beer.

'Of course,' she mused, 'that particular moment of recklessness might have been simply down to all that grappa.'

'Please don't mention the grappa,' he muttered, rubbing his chest and wincing. 'I can hardly bear thinking about it.'

She smiled at him with fond nostalgia. 'I'm not surprised, but then you were knocking it back like water.'

'Something had to make up for the dreadfully cheesy song you requested and then insisted on dancing to.'

She mentioned a famously cringe-worthy hit of the eighties and her eyebrows lifted. 'You told me it was your favourite.'

He shrugged. 'Desperate times call for desperate measures.'

'Were you really so keen to get me into bed?' she said, adding a touch of wistfulness that didn't sound entirely feigned.

'What do you think?'

'I think we were lucky the grappa didn't impede your performance.' She sent him a smile that shot straight through the length of him and curled his toes.

'Nor yours,' he murmured, finding it all too easy to vi-sualise Zoe on his bed and in his arms.

'All in all it was quite a night, wasn't it?' she said softly.

'It was.'

'Oh, this is *so* romantic,' sighed Harriet. 'Zoe told us you were the yin to her yang, the east to her west and the north to her south, and I can totally believe it. You two are totally made for each other.'

'We are, aren't we?' said Zoe, so warmly, so dreamily that for one horrible moment he thought she might actually mean it.

And if that wasn't enough to set off alarm bells, amid the collective female sighs, through the sudden haze in his head and above the rushing of the blood in his ears he heard Samantha coolly say, 'Zoe mentioned you were on the point of proposing, Dan, so tell us, when *are* you going to make an honest woman out of her?'

Oh, God, he thought, feeling a cold sweat breaking out all over his skin. How the hell could he have forgotten about that? When Zoe had brought it up, it hadn't seemed relevant because he hadn't planned on things going this far. But they had, and now he was going to have to propose because he couldn't walk out and leave her hanging now. Having come so far it really wouldn't be fair. Besides, he'd promised himself he'd see this thing through right to the end, and that was what he'd do.

Whether he'd be able to make it convincing, however, was an entirely different matter. An engagement of any sort wasn't something he'd ever really contemplated, at least not recently. So he'd just have to do it plainly and quickly, as if he couldn't wait to whisk Zoe off to celebrate prop-erly and in private.

The words he never imagined he'd hear himself say were on the tip of his tongue when Zoe got there first. 'Oh, he isn't,' she said a second before he said, 'She's right.'

Zoe's eyebrows shot up and he couldn't blame her because even he didn't know why he hadn't taken the out she'd given him. It had been tight but there'd been time, and one would have thought he'd have learned.

'She is?' she said faintly.

'Well, it *has* been six months, and I *am* the yin to your yang.'

She swallowed hard. 'What are you doing?'

'Isn't it obvious?'

'You know, you *really* don't have to do this.'

'Don't I?' he said wryly. It seemed to him he did.

'No.'

'Now that I think about it perhaps it *is* about time I made an honest woman out of you.'

She arched a sceptical eyebrow. 'It's way too late for that, don't you think?'

'It's never too late to do the right thing,' Dan said gravely, reminding her of her obligations now.

For a moment she considered. Then she nodded. 'OK,' she said, lifting her chin and taking a deep breath. 'Let's do it.'

He took her in her arms and pulled her close. 'Zoe Montgomery, will you marry me?'

'I'd love to.'

'Great.' He kissed her hard on the mouth. 'Now, are we done?' he said, staring down at her and thinking that now was definitely *finally* the time to leave.

'*God*, yes,' she said shakily.

'Then let's get out of here.'

Thank *heavens* that was all over, thought Zoe, slipping her arms through the sleeves of the coat that Dan was holding out and wondering if the shiver that ran down her spine was due to the chill of the evening or the fleeting brush of his fingers against her neck.

She didn't think she'd ever experienced so many emotions in the space of such a short time and wasn't sure she wanted to ever again because she was still trembling from the great tangled mess churning around her insides.

It was actually quite a surprise she was still standing. There'd been a point when Dan had clearly decided to up the ante on the charade front, and what with all those little squeezes and kisses he'd bestowed on her and the warm smiles and the hot looks he'd given her her legs had gone all shaky while her stomach had dissolved, and she'd thanked God that he'd had such a firm hold on her.

She'd been even more grateful of it when the litany of women in his life had been mentioned and a totally irrational shaft of white-hot jealousy had scythed through her, nearly wiping out her knees. That had just been weird and not a little disturbing because none of this evening had been for real and she really shouldn't have been affected by any of it.

She wasn't a fantasist, she reminded herself, making a start on doing up her buttons and trying not to stare at the sliver of taut tanned stomach that was briefly exposed just above the waistband of his jeans when Dan shrugged on his own jacket and his shirt rode up. She was a realist.

And yet ever since he'd taken her in his arms and 'proposed' she'd been secretly wondering what it would be like to feel like that for real. To have someone feel like that about her for real, to want to marry her for real…

Shaking her head to dispel the uncharacteristic flight of fancy, Zoe pulled herself together. She was being absurd. She was exhausted, probably. Hormonal, possibly. Stressed out, definitely. And that was why she was casting a man she barely knew in the role of white knight.

Maybe, though, she could get to know him a bit better, she thought, fixing the last of her buttons and feeling her spirits perk up at the idea that this needn't be goodnight.

Maybe she could buy him a drink to say thank you for helping her out. Maybe they could move on to dinner. And maybe they could see what happened after that.

OK, so she'd never actually asked anyone out before, but honestly, after months of disastrous on-line dating experiences and after everything she'd been through this evening that was hardly the Mount Everest of challenges, was it? He was single, she was single and they clearly fancied the pants off each other.

So she could do this, she told herself, her pulse now racing so fast it was beginning to make her dizzy. The advantages of asking him out vastly outweighed the disadvantages. Back in the bar he'd said he hadn't wanted to let her go, so the odds of him saying yes were stacked hugely in her favour. The risk of potential humiliation was so minimal as to be negligible. She had nothing to lose and everything to gain.

Nevertheless as she turned to face him her mouth went dry, a ball of nerves stuck in her throat and no amount of swallowing hard did anything to alleviate either. 'I can't thank you enough for your help,' she said a little huskily.

Straightening his lapels and then fixing his shirt collar, Dan looked over at her and gave her a faint smile. 'You're welcome.'

'You were amazing.'

'Not half as amazing as you. Did you really think up all that stuff on the spot?'

'The general premise I borrowed from my sister and her ex, but some of the details might have got a bit distorted.' The feelings were all her own though…

'Well, in a weird kind of way it was fun.'

'Yes, it was, wasn't it?' She smiled. 'You really didn't have to propose, though.'

'I thought it rounded things off rather nicely.'

'It did.'

He tugged at the cuffs of his shirt beneath the sleeves of his jacket and glanced up at her. 'So was it worth it?'

'The whole charade thing? I don't know yet. I guess I'll have to process it all and see.'

'It doesn't seem to me that they're worth wasting any more energy on.'

Hmm. 'Were you bullied at school?' she asked.

'No.'

Of course he wasn't; why would he be? 'Then it's easy for you to say.'

He shoved his hands in the pockets of his jeans and shrugged. 'Maybe. But my sister was. Bullies are generally cowards and Samantha's no different.'

'She's a bitch.'

'She is. She's also jealous of you.'

A moment's silence fell as Zoe stared at him in speechless astonishment. '*She's* jealous of *me*?'

He nodded. 'Deeply.'

'What on earth would she have to be jealous about?'

'Well, you're beautiful, brainy and successful, so there's a start.'

Once again Dan's words struck her dumb, only this time it wasn't astonishment that flooded through her but delicious languorous warmth. Did he really think her all that?

'I should also think she'd give her eye-teeth to have half your entrepreneurial spirit,' he continued with a little conspiratorial smile that did even crazier things to her temperature, 'because I happen to know that the Shipley Estate is broke.'

'Oh dear, is it?' she said, knowing that even without the distraction of the heat swirling through her veins she'd have failed to drum up much sympathy. 'Badly?'

'Stonily.'

'Hah,' she said instinctively then blushed. 'Sorry. That's not very charitable, is it?'

'But entirely justifiable.'

The conspiratorial smile deepened and his eyes kind of twinkled and her head began to swim at the realisation that for the first time in longer than she could remember someone was wholly on her side. *He'd* been on her side. Pretty much all evening.

So determinedly putting Samantha and her cronies from her mind, Zoe took a deep breath and braced herself because *they* might not be worth wasting her energy on but Dan very possibly might be.

'Look, Dan,' she said, sounding far cooler than she felt with all the stuff hurtling round inside her, 'would you like to go for a proper drink or get a bite to eat or something?'

He paused, arched an eyebrow at her and grinned. 'Are you asking me out on a date?'

Despite all her earlier self-assurances, at the hint of amusement in his voice her confidence in his answer and herself suddenly faltered, and Zoe felt her cheeks redden with enough warmth to heat the whole of London. 'I guess I am.'

'But we're engaged. Don't you think it's a bit late for that?'

'Would you mind just answering the question?' Preferably before she expired of either anticipation or overheating.

'Well, I'd love to—' he began before coming to an abrupt stop mid-sentence, frowning and shifting his gaze to a spot behind her and in that second smashing to smithereens all her stupid fragile hopes of normality, all her pathetically deluded ideas of romance and all her faith in statistics and probability as he did so. 'But—'

'Forget it,' she muttered before he could get in with the brush-off she'd naively never expected but with hindsight really should have done.

'No,' he said, snapping his attention back to her and whipping out a hand that she just about managed to dodge.

'I should get going.'

'Wait.'

'Dan! At last!'

At the sound of the voice behind her she stopped trying to avoid the efforts Dan was making to get her to stand still and spun round to see a tall broad man striding along the pavement towards them.

And then as a dozen different realisations cascaded into her brain the mortification that was already swilling around inside her surged up to fill every cell of her body and if she'd thought the warmth in her cheeks could have heated London before, now it could have kept the entire country nice and toasty throughout the winter.

Oh God, how could she have got it so badly wrong? Of *course* Dan wouldn't be wanting to have a drink with her. Of course he'd been in that pub to meet someone. Other people—especially people like him—had *friends*, didn't they? They had plans. And ones that didn't involve conjuring up fictitious boyfriends and concocting ludicrous relationships.

And wasn't he someone in the public eye? Someone very possibly famous, who had dozens of smokescreens slash girlfriends? What had she been *thinking*? Why on earth would a man with his charisma, his confidence and his looks want to go on a date with a basket case like her in any case? God, she was an idiot.

And how on earth could she have been so foolish as to have forgotten that none of those lovely affectionate kisses and squeezes in the pub had been real? That they'd all been for the benefit of their audience and all indirectly at her behest?

Why, oh why, had she ever opened that bloody email in the first place? Why hadn't she just left it in the trash? Why had she had to try and prove something?

More pressingly, why couldn't the ground open beneath

her feet and provide her with a great big Zoe-shaped hole she could conveniently disappear into?

'Sorry, sorry,' said the newcomer, sounding faintly out of breath as he shook Dan's hand and clapped him in a matey way on the back while Zoe wondered whether either of them would notice if she fell to the pavement and started head-butting it in an attempt to knock some sense back into her brain. 'My tube broke down and we sat in a bloody tunnel for hours. I reckoned I'd probably missed you. Good to see you're still here.' He turned to Zoe, eyeing her up and down, and a slow smile began to spread across his face. 'Who's this?'

'Pete Baker, Zoe Montgomery,' said Dan, still frowning as he waved a hand between the two of them.

'Who's just leaving,' she said, now wanting nothing more than to turn and run and carry her and her humiliation as far away as possible.

'Really?' said the man called Pete. 'Won't you stay and join us for a drink?'

And prolong the suffering? *God*, no. 'Thanks, but I really must be off. Work to do… You know…' She turned to Dan and grabbed his hand. 'Thanks again for everything,' she said, giving it a vigorous shake before letting it go. 'Enjoy the rest of your evening.'

And with that she flashed them both what she could only imagine was a truly manic smile, spun on her heel and practically ran for the station.

CHAPTER FIVE

DAN WAS SITTING at his kitchen table with his third espresso of the exceptionally early morning, frustrating himself hugely by staring blankly at the report he'd requested into the pros and cons of acquiring an agency that had recently come up for sale in the States, when his phone rang.

'So what's this I hear about my big brother finally biting the bullet and getting engaged?'

At his sister's conversational opener Dan jerked and nearly choked on his coffee. Other people might have started with a *hello, how are you* before launching into an interrogation, but not Celia. There was no beating about the bush for her. No second of her busy life wasted. And absolutely no mistaking a spade for anything other than a spade.

'What?' he said hoarsely, clearing his throat as he set his cup down and then thumping his chest.

'En-gaged,' his sister said again, only this time drawing out each syllable as if he was a little on the slow side. Which he was, hence the rocket-fuel-strength coffee. 'Last night. You…A girl…A pub, of all places, and a proposal… Does that ring any bells or has too much celebratory champagne annihilated your memory?'

Ring any bells? God. Dan planted his elbows on his desk and rubbed his eyes with the hand that wasn't clamping the phone to his ear because an entire churchful of the bloody things had been clanging in his head all sodding morning and he was getting thoroughly sick of it.

Unfortunately for his mood—which generally needed eight hours of sleep to function positively and had only had three—and his productivity—which generally needed a clear-headedness that was today conspicuous by its absence—there was nothing whatsoever wrong with his memory. On the contrary, over the past twelve hours or so it had been working better than ever, making a complete mockery of his attempts to put the events of last night, the kisses, Zoe and her bizarre exit in particular, out of his mind and get some sleep.

'One or two,' he muttered, not for the first time regretting that he'd only managed a non-oblivion-inducing two pints with Pete before they'd called it a night.

'So, go on, then, spill the beans. If this Zoe Montgomery mystery shopper statistician person is going to be my sister-in-law, I want to know *everything*. Like where did you meet her? How long have you known her? Why have you never mentioned her? And will you be bringing her to Oliver's wedding?'

Dan was just about to rattle the answers off in the same quick-fire way the questions had come at him—the pub, twelve hours, because he'd only recently been made aware of her existence and not before hell froze over—when he suddenly sat up and went still.

Hang on. Where the hell had Celia got such detailed information? In fact, how did she know *anything*? It was seven in the morning. Surely the grapevine hadn't been active all night.

'How do you know so much about it?' he said, not at all sure he was ready to hear the answer.

His sister tutted and he could imagine her rolling her eyes. 'Don't you ever read the papers?'

And just like that, Dan froze. A bead of sweat trickled

down his bare back and a wave of nausea rolled through him as the coffee turned his stomach. Oh, God, he thought, his skin going all clammy and his head beginning to pound. No. Not again. It couldn't have happened again. Could it?

'Celia?' he said, his voice sounding thick and distant beneath the roar in his ears. 'I'll have to call you back.'

One quick Google search and five minutes later Dan was face to face with the irrefutable evidence that it had.

Every one of the concerns about the wisdom of going along with Zoe's plan that he'd considered and stupidly dismissed had been justified because there, stretching right across the screen of his laptop, was the bold black headline that practically salivated as it shouted 'Has London's Most Eligible Bachelor Been Snagged?!' Beneath it was a picture of him and Zoe kissing—that second time—clearly so involved, so caught up in the heat and the passion of the moment that that time he hadn't noticed the flash of the camera.

And then beneath *that* was the article.

It started with a brief paragraph about the events of the latter part of the previous evening. It segued into a section about Zoe in which he learned that she had a doctorate in statistics from one of the country's top universities and was co-managing director of Montgomery Mystery Shopping Limited with her sister, Lily. Then followed line upon line of rehashed detail about his career history and his eligibility, the story Jasmine had sold and the usual one-woman-a-week crap.

Practically the only relationship it *didn't* mention, he thought grimly, the only relationship that had *never* been mentioned anywhere in fact, was the one he'd had with Natalie Blake when he was in his mid-twenties, the one that had shattered his ability to trust women and sent him hurtling off the rails. And the only reason that *that* hadn't made it into the headlines was because firstly it had taken place before either of them had become of interest to the press, and secondly what with Natalie's subsequent mete-oric rise to supermodel stardom it wouldn't do her repu-tation any good if it got out that she'd aborted his baby in order to pursue her career.

So who was responsible for *this*? he wondered, steering his thoughts back before they could head down that partic-ular dark and gloomy track. Zoe? One of the other women there? Did it matter?

There was little point in being disappointed that his sus-picions and concerns had been confirmed. Little point in beating himself up about his stupidity last night or berating himself for not paying attention to the voice of reason that had constantly been telling him to take a deep breath and step away. Even less in wondering whether he had his reck-less streak quite as under control as he'd always assumed.

What mattered now was damage limitation, thought Dan, shoving his hands through his hair and rubbing his eyes to wipe out any lingering woolly-headedness, because if he didn't keep his wits about him and concentrate on clearing up the mess that his rash act of chivalry seemed to have caused his life could get very complicated indeed.

Sitting back in his chair, he contemplated the two ways he could go from here and speedily narrowed it down to one because as far as he was concerned continuing with the charade was not an option.

For one thing, what would be the point? He had no need whatsoever for a fake fiancée and nothing to gain from having one. For another, the existence of such a figure in his life would only unfairly raise his mother's hopes, and things could easily escalate to the point where he found himself manipulated into waiting for his fake fiancée at a genuine altar.

And as for Zoe, well, she'd tried to dissuade him from

proposing in the first place, so couldn't he reasonably assume that outside her school reunion she had as much need for a fake fiancé as he did?

He could, and OK, yes, etiquette probably demanded that he at least let her know he was breaking off their 'engagement', but etiquette didn't take Celia into consideration. Having known his sister for thirty-one of his thirty-three years, he knew he had to nip things in the bud right now, because if he fudged things, if he attempted to put her off, she'd instantly leap to completely the wrong conclusion and then the grapevine—not to mention his mother—really would be quivering.

Besides it was seven a.m. and all he'd be able to find on the Internet would be Zoe's work contact details, and even if she was a workaholic as she'd implied he doubted she'd be in the office this early. So he'd just have to wait before calling her and hope he got to her before anyone else did.

Picking up the phone and bracing himself for an uncomfortable couple of calls, Dan set his jaw and vowed that if ever the opportunity to indulge his chivalrous streak arose again, if ever a beautiful woman batted her eyelids up at him and begged him to do her a favour, if ever he thought he could get the better of fate, he'd ignore the whole bloody lot of it.

When Zoe's mobile rang a while after Dan had wound up his extensive damage limitation exercise and done as much as he could to clear up the mess with various press and familial interests, she was head down and utterly absorbed in the work she was doing, her coffee going cold while she clicked her mouse on cell after cell and her brain sifted through the data in front of her.

So as she fumbled for the phone and stuck it to her ear she was totally unprepared for what was about to come.

'Hello?' she muttered distractedly, frowning at a column

of figures and trying to work out why they weren't adding up the way she'd expected.

'Hi, Zoe?'

At the sound of the silky voice at the other end of the line all the little hairs at the back of her neck shot up and Zoe went still, numerical anomalies instantly forgotten as memories of last night flooded into her head. Memories she actually thought she'd done a pretty good job of suppressing, since last night was *not* a night she'd be looking back on with fond nostalgia, but evidently hadn't.

Determinedly ignoring the wave of emotion that reared up inside her and banking down the apprehension that instinctively skidded through her, Zoe took a deep steadying breath and reminded herself for what felt like the hundredth time that last night had been nothing more than a blip in her otherwise totally logical and rational existence; that she was thirty-two, not sixteen; and that she could handle whatever the morning had to throw at her.

Even Samantha Newark.

'Samantha,' she said with a pleasing degree of cool control. 'Good morning. How are you?'

'On tremendous form,' said Samantha. 'Wasn't last night fun?'

Hmm. Fun wasn't quite the word she'd have used to describe the maelstrom of madness that the evening had become, but small talk she could do. Heaven knew she'd been practising long enough. 'Absolutely hilarious,' she said dryly.

'And so very dramatic, what with Dan's proposal.'

As the memory of being in his arms and then locking lips with him broke free and slammed into her head, Zoe went warm and thanked heavens that this conversation wasn't being conducted face to face. 'Well, that's Dan for you,' she said, sounding mercifully normal. 'He never does anything by half.'

'He certainly doesn't.'

At Samantha's oddly knowing tone, Zoe tensed for a second and then forced herself to relax. 'So what can I do for you?' she asked, even though something told her that based on past experience it wouldn't be anything good.

'I was just calling to see how you were,' said Samantha, her voice dripping with insincere concern.

'Me?' said Zoe, ignoring the 'concern' and concentrating on how she might feel were she really engaged to Dan and imagining she'd be rather pleased. 'Oh, I'm deliriously happy.'

There was a pause. 'Really?'

'Really.'

'Well, I must say I'm surprised.'

'Why?'

'I'd have thought under the circumstances you'd be devastated.'

Zoe frowned. 'Under what circumstances?' she asked, curiosity overriding her sense of self-preservation.

'Your broken engagement naturally.'

Her heart skipped a beat and for some reason her stomach fell. 'My broken engagement?'

'Don't tell me you didn't know?' said Samantha with what Zoe could only describe as morbid glee.

Of course she didn't know, she would have announced if the person she was talking to was anyone other than Samantha. Why on earth would she? She hadn't heard from Dan, and after her excruciatingly embarrassing overreaction to Pete's arrival and the extraordinary way she'd run off like that she didn't expect to. Plus she'd been so engrossed in work she'd deliberately ignored the phone all morning until in her confusion she'd made the mistake of answering her mobile. And she certainly wasn't going to ask Samantha where she'd found out that piece of information and give her nemesis the satisfaction of telling her.

Besides the how, when and why of it didn't matter. All that mattered right now was that Zoe had left the pub with something of the upper hand for the first time in her life, and Samantha had somehow managed to wrestle it back from her. The evil cow was once again in a position to hurt her, laugh at her and generally make her morning a misery, and there was no question that she was going to do it.

As Zoe's heart sank all the old feelings of inadequacy surged up inside her and she automatically began to work out how to backtrack and extricate herself from this conversation with a modicum of dignity. She racked her brains for some sort of explanation and scrabbled around for an excuse and when that failed frantically sought the wherewithal to brush it all off as if she didn't give a toss and then hang up.

As the seconds ticked by and she still didn't have a clue how to deal with this Zoe felt the desperation and humiliation churning around inside her escalate. Her head swam and the desperation turned to panic and a wave of nausea clutched at her stomach.

And then, quite suddenly, mid-brainstorm, mid-panic, she stopped.

Hang on, she thought, sitting bolt upright and staring straight ahead. Why the hell was she doing this? Still? It had been fifteen years, for heaven's sake. *Fifteen years*. Would she still be trying to twist herself into someone else in another fifteen? Would she still be apologising and cowering and fighting for her dignity?

At the uncomfortable awareness that all this was entirely possible unless she did something about it now, Zoe shuddered. No, she thought, setting her jaw and rallying her inner troops. She wasn't going to let this continue. She couldn't. She had to finish this once and for all. Dan had been right: if she stood any chance of moving on she really did.

And what was it he'd said on the pavement outside the

pub last night? Samantha and her friends weren't worth wasting any more energy on? Well, dammit, he was right about that too. She'd already wasted far too much energy and time in her youth trying to be something she wasn't and apologising for the person she was.

Who were they anyway? She didn't even like them. She'd spent pretty much all her teenage years secretly and perversely in awe of them, trying to do her damnedest to fit in, when actually they weren't worth fitting in with. In fact, as was so often the case with bullies, *they* were the ones who were lacking, the ones to be pitied, not her.

Resisting the urge to kick herself for not coming to this devastating conclusion fifteen years ago when it really could have made a difference, Zoe pulled herself together and cleared her head so she could focus and take control of a relationship that had been far too one-sided for far too long, and then put an end to it.

'Why would I know?' she asked calmly, feeling oddly liberated as the panic and nausea fell away.

'Well, you *were* the fiancée.'

'And seeing as how the whole thing was a set-up in the first place why would I even care?'

'A set-up?' echoed Samantha, sounding taken aback.

'That's right.'

'You mean the proposal?'

'I mean the whole lot of it.'

'I don't understand.'

Having Samantha on the back foot for once caused an unstoppable sense of empowerment to rise up inside her. 'There was no boyfriend, no grappa and no ski-resort naughtiness,' she said almost giddily. 'I made it all up.'

There was a moment's stunned silence as this clearly startling revelation sank in. 'But what about Dan?'

'I met him about half an hour before you did and asked him to help me out.'

Samantha might have been momentarily thrown but it didn't take her long to recover. 'Hah, I knew it,' she said triumphantly. 'I knew you'd never manage to tie a man like him down.'

'I doubt anyone will,' said Zoe, determinedly ignoring the barb and thinking instead about the way he'd tensed when she'd mentioned they'd been going out for six months.

'You were always so independent...and *such* a control-freak.' Samantha made both sound like the worst character traits on the planet and Zoe couldn't help bristling all over again because as far as she was concerned there was absolutely nothing wrong with being responsible for yourself or wanting to be in control of you life.

'I still am,' she said.

'You never were very good at holding onto men, were you?'

'No, well, you made sure of that, didn't you, Samantha?' The night of their leaving dance, in fact, when Zoe had finally plucked up the courage to invite a boy from the village where her parents lived that she'd had a crush on for ages. She'd been so excited she hadn't properly thought through the possible ramifications. If she had she might have been prepared for Samantha to sidle over and mock her date in front of him and she might have been prepared for her to then snog him in the middle of the dance floor an hour later, but then again she might not.

'Oh, come on,' said Samantha with a sneer. 'You're not still smarting about that, are you?'

'No more than you are that Dan didn't respond to any of your flirting last night.'

There was a pause while Samantha took the shot and rallied. 'Did you know he's one of the most eligible bachelors in London?'

'I didn't, but I can quite see why.'

'He's at number two on Tatler's Little Black Book list.'

'Only at number two?' she exclaimed in mock horror. 'Who's at number one?'

'Royalty.'

'Naturally.'

'So what would he see in you?'

'Well, quite,' she agreed, although actually he had seen something in her, hadn't he? Something that had made him kiss her as if his life depended on it, something that had set his heart thumping and his hands trembling and his body hardening where it mattered, and something she really should have taken into account before fleeing last night, because for all she knew the 'but' she'd sensed coming might not have been the brush-off she'd assumed but a 'but I'm a bit tied up at the moment so how about I take your number and give you a call?'. Damn, she needed to address the issues she had with self-esteem...

'Bit sad, though, to invent a boyfriend, don't you think?'

'Completely pathetic,' she said, dragging her concentration away from Dan's physical attributes and her abandonment of logic and applying it to the conversation. 'And way below me.'

'So why do it?'

'Heaven knows,' she said, because she might be willing to offload the truth about last night but there was such a thing as going too far, and confessing to many and highly personal insecurities to this woman definitely ventured into that territory.

'Trying to impress us, were you?' said Samantha mockingly.

'Very probably. And you were, weren't you? Impressed, I mean.'

Samantha sniffed. 'Hardly.'

'Anyway, it really doesn't matter any more,' said Zoe, setting her jaw and pulling her shoulders back because if ever there was a time for a steely backbone this was it.

'For a while last night I totally lost my mind but that's fine because now I'm back in possession of it, and you know something, Samantha, you might have made my life pretty damn miserable for the best part of seven years, but not any longer. I've had enough. I truly don't care what you think about me. I haven't seen you in fifteen years, and I doubt I will again in the next fifteen. You do not matter to me. Your opinion of me does not matter to me. Nothing you say or do has any effect on me any more. It's over.'

And with that she hung up, relief pouring through her and her teenage self whooping and cheering in the background.

The pride and delight Zoe felt at finally standing up to the silly cow and telling her to get lost lasted about an hour.

She'd hung up, and done a happy dance in her chair, wishing that Lily were here to celebrate her new-found freedom instead of being halfway up a mountain checking out a corporate bonding package on behalf of a new client, and out of contact. Positively zinging with euphoria and adrenalin, she'd spotted the numerical anomaly almost instantly and had handled a couple of client emails she would otherwise have left for her more client-friendly sister.

But then she'd found herself going over the phone call in her head, and she kept coming back to what Samantha had said about not being able to hold onto a man. Whether she'd intended to or not, Samantha had hit on one of Zoe's weakest spots—and not just because it had brought back memories of her crush at eighteen.

As much as it pained her to admit it Samantha had a point. She *was* hopeless at holding onto a man. Three months was her longest relationship, and for a woman of thirty-two that wasn't exactly anything to write home about.

Her last attempt had ended a month ago when Mike had dumped her and a six-week relationship had bitten the dust. Why she still bothered to try and have one of the bloody things when she was so useless at them was anyone's guess, but some pathetically optimistic part of her constantly hoped that *this* one would be different. That *this* man would be strong enough to put up with her idiosyncrasies and insecurities, and interesting and attractive enough for her to put up with his.

Well, Mike certainly hadn't been any of that, not that he'd stuck around long enough for either of them to find out for sure.

Utterly fed up with her run of bad luck Zoe had tossed in the online dating towel and had tried her damnedest to forget the whole humiliating experience of their break-up, but Mike's parting shot had lodged in her brain and infuriatingly refused to budge.

Moments before throwing his hands in the air and declaring that he was giving up, he'd accused her of being a workaholic number-cruncher who was boring and unimaginative and less fun than a burst appendix, and naturally enough, when she'd thought things had been going rather well for a change, it had stung.

Even worse, when she'd told her sister what he'd said Lily had tentatively suggested that maybe, just maybe, Mike had had a very small point and that perhaps she should think about getting a life beyond the company, and that had stung even more.

Lily had even remarked that Zoe might like to find a hobby, which at the time had made Zoe snort with derision because, really? A *hobby*? Where would she find the time for a hobby? Besides, statistical analysis *was* her hobby, which was handy seeing as how their business involved such a lot of it.

Consoling herself with the thought that Mike had had a very small point indeed and hadn't been particularly good with it, and reminding herself that as the company already had one zany and creative but numerically challenged co-owner in Lily her own skill-set and dedication were vital, Zoe had calmly brushed the criticism aside with a couldn't-care-less shrug and had decided to move on.

But to her frustration moving on had proved easier said than done, and over the last few weeks she'd found herself dwelling on what Mike and Lily had said, analysing her life from angles she'd never previously considered, and had wound up wondering whether her ex and her sister might not actually be right.

She *did* channel pretty much every waking hour she had into the business, and, while in the beginning it had been necessary for survival, the company was so well established now and so successful she probably didn't need to keep her foot on the accelerator *all* the time.

And as constantly working had become such a habit maybe she had become even more of a hermit than usual. The handful of times Mike had tried to drag her out to dinner or a party she'd acquiesced with such bad grace and then slunk around in the background in an effort to avoid anyone who looked as if they might want to chat that with the benefit of hindsight she couldn't entirely blame him for giving up on her.

So maybe her inability to hold down a man *was* her fault, she thought now, picking up her mug and grimacing at the mouthful of horribly cold coffee she ended up with and the sticky skin that clung to her lips. Maybe what had happened at school had squashed her self-esteem and self-confidence so much that she *did* go into every relationship thinking it was doomed from the start. She certainly didn't bother to fight for them much.

Oh, she could try and console herself with a whole bunch of statistics about the odds of divorce and that her highly valued reason and logic held no truck with anything as unquantifiable as love, but hadn't she perhaps been kidding herself all these years? Wasn't it more likely to be that she couldn't let her guard down with men in case they discovered the mess she was beneath the cool and confident professional exterior?

And if that *was* the case, she thought, pushing away from her desk and getting up to go and make a fresh cup of coffee, and her disaster of a love-life *had* been a sort of indirect result of the bullying, then seeing as how she'd just put *that* to bed so to speak wouldn't that mean she could now do something to remedy the situation? Because now she was free to build up her self-esteem and confidence and become the person she thought she could be on a personal as well as professional level.

She'd been told she needed to get a life. Well, maybe it was about time she did, because she was now thinking that she must be incredibly hard work to go out with and it was no wonder no man had stuck around for long.

Maybe it was time to drop her guard, she thought, her heart thumping a little bit faster. Maybe she should let loose and see what happened. And even if a relationship didn't land in her lap right away, maybe she could just have some fun for a change. She was thirty-two for heaven's sake. Surely she ought to have had some seriously good sex by now, either within or without a relationship.

Zoe sat back down at her desk before her knees gave way at the thought of mind-bending earth-shattering sex.

Ideally with Dan, she thought suddenly, heat racing through her veins. He looked like he knew how to have fun. He'd kissed her with more than just perfunctory passion, and she'd felt the evidence that he was attracted to her. Lord knew she was attracted to him. She might not know a huge amount about it but if the heat that they could generate just from kissing was anything to go by, then the sex would be out of this world.

He'd be good for her self-esteem too. Quite apart from

obviously wanting her, when he'd told her she was brainy and beautiful her spirits had soared. If she were a betting woman, which she wasn't given how the odds were so often stacked against the average punter, then she'd bet that Dan would help to build up her confidence beautifully. Indirectly he might even help her to find the real her that she could feel was buried beneath a whole heap of self-doubt, vulnerability and fear.

So maybe, thought Zoe, looking up the contact details of DBF Associates online and feeling adrenalin begin to surge through her, just maybe, if she asked, Dan might be up for having some fun with her.

CHAPTER SIX

IT WAS NOW or never.

Zoe hovered at the door of the hotel ballroom she'd been lurking around for the past ten minutes, watching Dan and the party of people he was with—his staff, presumably—diverge to the bar, her heart beating like a drum and her blood pounding through her veins.

Now she was actually here she wasn't entirely sure it was a good idea. It had seemed like one when she'd come up with the plan earlier this afternoon and plucked up enough guts to dress herself up and make her way to the central London hotel where some advertising award ceremony was being held and where she'd been told that Dan would be.

Right up until the taxi had deposited her at the front door she'd managed to maintain a sense of calm and just about hold onto her equilibrium, but the minute she'd laid eyes on him all that had vanished and now a dangerous cocktail of nerves, desire and recklessness was swilling around inside her making her feel edgy and wild.

If she'd thought he'd looked good last night it wasn't a patch on the devastation he was wreaking on her senses with the black-dinner-jacket-white-shirt combo he was wearing tonight.

Gorgeous didn't even begin to cover it. The suit fitted him so perfectly it must have been made for him. The snowy whiteness of his shirt made his hair and eyes look even darker, and now he was tugging his bow tie undone and undoing the top button of his shirt, which gave him a kind of rakish, dishevelled air that made her heart beat even faster.

But it wasn't just the way he looked. There was an edge about him too this evening that she could sense even from way over here. He looked as smoulderingly dangerous as she felt, and remarkably tense for someone who'd just won a highly acclaimed award.

For a moment her confidence in her plan to accost him here, which she'd thought fairly foolproof at the time, faltered. Dan's unexpected edginess—and her own—gave the evening a potential unpredictability that she hadn't prepared for and the whole evening could backfire.

Plus she was belatedly realising that Dan was here in a professional capacity, among his colleagues, his peers and his competitors, and it was entirely possible that the last thing he'd want would be her bounding up to him telling him she wanted him.

So maybe she should leave and drop in on Monday morning instead, she thought, nibbling on her lip while her resolve to go through with this wavered. Maybe she'd been a complete and utter idiot to turn up here like this. Dan was busy. She was going through a period of serious mental instability. This would never work. She must have been mad to even think it might.

She took a step back and the tight band around her chest eased. It looked as if it was going to be never. Which was fine. Dan probably wouldn't want to hook up with her anyway.

Zoe was about to take another step back, turn on her heel and leave the way she came in when she stopped.

Hang on, she thought. No. This plan had been the right one. There were reasons she'd come up with it. And she might not remember them all right now but she was pretty sure they were good ones too. So she wasn't going to wimp out. Again. She was going to find her metaphorical balls and relocate the thrill that his edginess had caused to ripple through her, because this was an opportunity she really shouldn't ignore.

So it wasn't going to be never, thought Zoe, lifting her chin and pulling her shoulders back. It was going to be now.

Dan gritted his teeth and thought that if anyone else congratulated him on his 'engagement' he might very well lose what was now only a tenuous grip on his temper.

He'd thought he'd done more than enough to stem the tide of speculation. He'd fended off his sister and set his mother straight in what had to have been one of the most emotionally stressful conversations of his life. He'd contacted the newspaper and issued a denial. He'd instructed his secretary and receptionist to put any journalist who might call or pitch up right, and he'd asked one of his staff to handle the social media side of things too.

But the message didn't seem to have spread fast enough and he was sick of having to explain the whole misunderstanding.

He was also sick of the way that it meant that he was constantly reminded of it, of Zoe, and the effect she was still having on him. Even though he hadn't laid eyes on her in nearly twenty-four hours—and hopefully wouldn't ever again because last night he'd totally forgotten how practically every bloody thing he did at the moment ended up in the press and it couldn't be allowed to happen again—he couldn't get her out of his head, and this level of distraction, of fixation, was getting beyond a joke.

Of all the nights to be feeling so edgy and out of sorts this shouldn't have been it. It wasn't every day his company won a major award for one of their campaigns, and it wasn't every day that his staff had a chance to truly let their hair down as a team.

After dinner and the actual ceremony they'd been the first to migrate to the bar and had taken up a position that was probably going to see them through until morning. Dan had stuck a credit card behind the bar and then the real hair-letting-down had begun, with everyone apart from him knocking back the booze as if it were about to run out, high on adrenalin and delight.

They'd all worked bloody hard over the last year and deserved this success, he realised more belatedly than he'd have liked. They deserved his appreciation too, and he couldn't blame them for giving him a wide berth.

So pulling himself together, he tapped his now empty glass and, once he had their attention, made a quick toast. Then to a smatter of applause, and a cheer or two, he apologised for being such a grumpy sod and ordered another bottle of champagne.

With single-minded focus he concentrated on the conversation, made himself laugh and joke with his colleagues until eventually he found the wherewithal to relax.

By and large he thought he was doing pretty well and that he'd be able to keep it up for another hour or so when he could head home and crash out. Until out of the corner of his eye he caught a flash of blonde hair, a shimmer of green and the trace of a scent his brain thought it recognised. Something about the combination made his fingers tighten round the stem of his glass, the laughter die in his throat and his entire body tighten with what he didn't know.

Surely Zoe wasn't here? She couldn't be. Why would she be? Closing his eyes, Dan took a deep breath and gave his head a quick shake. Then he opened his eyes and braced himself before glancing around just in case.

There was no sign of a blonde in a green dress. Of course there wasn't. But God, now he was *seeing* her? Smelling her? He might not trust women but he'd always been able to trust his instincts. If those were about to let him down as well, then what was left?

Dan set his jaw and gritted his teeth and wished he could rewind time and choose a different pub to meet Pete, because frankly the last twenty-four hours had been about as far removed from his generally smooth and calm existence as it was possible to be, and despite what he might like to tell himself his nerves were shredded.

So much so that he didn't know what he would be imagining next. Zoe right behind him? Her voice at his shoulder? Her touch on his arm?

And then he froze all over again because now he could hear her saying his name and feel her touching his arm and even his imagination wasn't that good. Which meant that he hadn't been wrong and that for some unfathomable reason she *was* here.

For a moment Dan felt a burst of satisfaction that his instincts hadn't failed, a surge of heat at the thought of her standing so close behind him, and an almost irresistible urge to whip round and drag her into his arms, all of which he instantly doused because if it got out who she was then he didn't stand *any* chance of being left alone tonight.

So, bracing himself, he turned slowly round and tried not to draw in a sharp breath as the full force of her effect unleashed itself on him.

That flash of green was in fact a tight strapless dress that moulded itself to her and showed off inches of lovely creamy skin. It was a stupendous piece of tailoring, he thought, running his gaze down her. It looked incredible on her but would look even better pooled at her feet in the shadows of his bedroom.

Gritting his teeth against the bolt of desire that rocked through him, Dan dragged his gaze back up but it didn't alleviate the tension gripping him. Her hair was up, pulled loosely back into some sort of fixture that allowed tendrils to curl around her face, and she was wearing the kind of make-up that made her eyes look all dark and smoky and smouldering and her mouth pale.

Overall it was a good look on her. A sexy look. The kind of look that made him think all she'd have to do was crook her little finger and he'd be right there, willingly going wherever she went and doing whatever she asked of him.

Which was *not* the idea, he reminded himself.

'What the hell are you doing here?' he muttered, telling himself to focus on what was important.

'I wanted to talk to you.'

'About what?'

She glanced around and frowned. 'Perhaps we could go somewhere a bit more private?'

'Great idea,' he murmured, checking that they weren't attracting attention, then taking her arm and leading her off.

The sooner he got her out of here, the better. The picture of them kissing had obscured her face, otherwise they'd be surrounded right about now, but who knew how long it would be before someone made the connection? In fact he ought to put her straight into a taxi and send her on her way because hadn't he thought only a little while ago that he didn't want to have anything to do with her ever again?

But instead he kept her close as he scanned the hotel lobby, not for the exit, but for a dark secluded spot well out of the way of prying eyes. And when he spied a couple of chairs partially hidden by a giant potted palm he didn't even think about why he wanted to hear what she had to say.

'This private enough for you?' he asked, once she'd arranged herself on the wicker chair and he'd flung himself into the one opposite.

'Perfect,' she said with a smile that scrambled his brain. 'Congratulations, by the way,' she added, leaning forwards, so intoxicatingly close and within reach that for a second he didn't have a clue what she was talking about.

'Thanks,' he said, eventually coming round to the realisation that she was referring to the award and not his mental descent into chaos. 'So why are you here, Zoe?'

'You weren't taking calls and when I turned up at your office earlier your receptionist said you weren't seeing visitors.'

'How did you know where I'd be?'

'She told me.'

Dan frowned. What the hell? His receptionist had given him a mushy little smile this morning and had muttered something about love's young dream before he'd put her straight but this kind of interference was going too far. Come Monday morning they'd be having words.

'Don't blame her,' said Zoe, reading his mind with alarming ease. 'I was rather persistent.'

'I can imagine,' he said dryly as the way she'd got him to help her out last night sprang to the front of his mind.

'It's a new talent I seem to have developed.'

'I didn't see you earlier.'

'No, well, I've only just arrived.' She turned a little shifty. 'I'm not exactly on the guest list.'

'Gatecrashing?' he said. 'I'm flattered.'

'You should be. That's *not* a talent I intend to develop.'

'Are there any others I should know about?'

She let those dark smoky eyes of hers drift down over him, and he felt his body respond wherever she lingered. His skin burned, his muscles tensed and he hardened where he had no business hardening in the middle of a work evening out. Then she slowly lifted her gaze, smiled slightly, as if she knew exactly the effect she was having on him and was wondering what she was going to do with it. 'Possibly,' she murmured.

Dan swallowed hard and curled one hand into a fist and

wrapped the other one around it in order to get rid of the itch to reach for her. 'You have heard we're no longer engaged, haven't you?' he said just in case she was here because of that.

'Oh, yes,' she said dryly. 'Samantha was very quick to ring with that piece of information.'

Dan inwardly winced. 'Didn't you get my voicemail?

'Voicemail?'

'I left a few.'

'Oh, well, no. I don't often answer the phone when I'm working. My sister Lily usually takes care of that, but she's away.'

'I'm sorry you had to hear it from Samantha.'

She waved a dismissive hand. 'Don't be. There's absolutely no need to apologise. In fact I rather think I should be thanking you.'

'What for?'

'I took your advice and finally told her where to get off.'

An unexpected bolt of admiration made him suddenly smile. 'How did she take it?'

'I didn't wait to find out.'

'And how are you taking it?'

'I feel extraordinarily liberated.'

She looked it. She looked sort of glowing. 'You look gorgeous,' he said gruffly.

She smiled. 'Thank you. So do you.'

For a moment they just stared at each other, their gazes locked together, until Zoe blinked and the connection broke. His heart beating oddly fast, Dan shoved a hand through his hair and swallowed. 'So what do you want, Zoe?'

She took a deep breath and looked him straight in the eye. 'OK, well, the thing is I rather think I want you.'

His heart practically stopped. 'What for?' he said, his imagination instantly conjuring up a dozen different possibilities before he reined it in, because surely she couldn't be wanting what *he* was wanting. No. It was probably advertising advice she wanted.

'Some fun,' she said, blowing that theory out of the water.

'Fun?'

'Well, it's sex I'm after, really.'

Dan nearly swallowed his tongue. 'Sex?'

If she noticed his lack of original vocabulary, she didn't mention it. Instead she looked at his mouth and nodded. 'Uh-huh.'

'With me?'

'That's right.'

'Anything else other than sex?'

She shrugged. 'Not especially. I don't mind either way.'

Barely able to believe he was having this conversation, Dan fought for composure. 'You don't seem the no-strings type.'

'I'm not. Or at least I haven't been. And that's rather the point.'

'What do you mean?'

'I've got stuck in a bit of a rut, and a pretty boring one at that. I've been working too hard. I need to get out of it before I fossilise. I'm thirty-two, Dan, and I've never really had truly amazing sex, and I want some.'

'What makes you think it would be truly amazing between us?'

God, what was he, stupid? Zoe merely arched an eyebrow as if in perfect agreement with his silent self-assessment.

'OK, forget that,' he muttered. 'Dumb question. How have you got to thirty-two without ever having had great sex?'

She shrugged and tellingly flickered her eyes away from his for a second. 'Oh, just unlucky, I guess.'

Some kind of sixth sense told him that there was more to it than that, but Dan was in no fit state to work out what, let alone begin an in-depth intelligent conversation about it, which was good because as he no longer did the sharing of personal information he wasn't particularly interested.

All he could think about was how incredibly gorgeous she looked, how great she'd felt last night, how bemused—and disappointed—he'd been by her dramatic flight from the pub, and how much he wanted her.

'So what do you think?' she prompted.

Dan's mouth went dry and his blood roared in his ears and his brain struggled to formulate any thought that didn't involve Zoe naked. If they slipped out the back and caught a taxi there, who would ever know? And God knew how long it had been since he'd had sex. 'You really want this?'

She nodded. 'Yes, if you do.'

'Oh, I do.'

She gave him a slow seductive smile. 'I was hoping you might say that.'

With his heart beating furiously and desire pounding through him Dan leapt to his feet, held out his hand and said, 'Then you'd better come with me.'

CHAPTER SEVEN

WHEN DAN MADE a decision he certainly didn't hang about, thought Zoe, sitting in the back of a taxi a quarter of an hour later. He hadn't even gone back inside to say goodbye to the people he'd been with. He'd just whisked her off to the cloakroom to retrieve their coats, then he'd bundled her into a taxi, given the driver his address and they were off.

And thank God for it because she'd been on the verge of spontaneously combusting for a while now and she wasn't sure how much longer she could contain herself. That electrifying conversation they'd had in the hotel lobby had been so hot she was surprised the wicker chair she'd been sitting in hadn't gone up in flames. At one point she'd even vaguely looked around for the location of the nearest fire extinguisher.

At the time she'd thought Dan had been equally affected—he'd certainly seemed as rapt by her as she'd been by him—and she'd half expected him to grab her the minute they'd got into the taxi.

But he hadn't. He'd immediately turned to stare out of the window and hadn't said a word since they'd pulled away so what was going through his mind now she had no idea.

Under normal circumstances Zoe didn't have a problem with silence. On the contrary, generally she was a huge fan of the stuff. But this silence was deafening and vibrating with a weird kind of tension and she felt as if she were sitting on knives. The edge to him she'd noticed earlier was still there, filling the foot or so between them in the taxi and making her stomach quiver with anticipation and her skin prickle.

It was all so excruciating, and growing even more so with every mile the taxi ate up that eventually Zoe couldn't stand the silence any longer. Clearing her throat, she turned slightly to face his profile.

'Did you know that the first white line in the road appeared in this country in nineteen twenty-one?' she said, her voice sounding weirdly loud in the inky darkness of the back of the taxi.

'What?' Dan muttered, not taking his eyes off whatever held his fascination, which really wasn't that much of a surprise since it was undoubtedly more interesting than her stab at conversation.

Not that she cared about that particularly. Given that exhibitionism had never been part of her plan, as far as she was concerned anything was better than the alternative of jumping into his lap and wrapping herself around him, and, as numbingly boring and unsexy as traffic planning might be, the more she concentrated on the lines in the road, the less she thought about the lines of his thighs and the less her fingers itched with the urge to get acquainted with them.

'The first white line in the road appeared in this country in nineteen twenty-one,' she said again and silently dared him to look at her.

'Did it?'

'It did. Such a simple thing,' she mused, 'and yet did you know that white lines can save up to eight times as many lives as a speed trap?'

'Can they?'

'So the statistics show. Filter lanes can reduce accidents by as much as twenty per cent on some stretches of road.'

'How interesting,' he said, sounding as though he thought it anything but.

'I find it fascinating,' she said, 'but then I find any kind of statistical analysis fascinating.'

'So it would seem.'

At the tightness of his voice and the flatness of his tone, Zoe frowned. Dan hadn't budged an inch. He was still sitting there with his arms folded staring resolutely out of the window, his jaw tight and his brow furrowed.

In light of her less than scintillating conversation, was he regretting his decision to take her home? It was entirely possible, of course, but she wasn't giving up without at least a bit of a fight. So what might he find interesting? she wondered. What would capture his attention and get him to look at her?

She racked her brains for a moment before seeing a billboard flash past and having something of a light-bulb moment.

'Take underwear, for example,' she said.

There was the tiniest of pauses. 'Underwear?' he said.

'Women's underwear in particular.'

She thought she heard him blow out a breath. 'What about it?' he muttered.

'When men buy their wives or girlfriends underwear, seventy per cent of them go for red lace with bows and stuff hanging off it and holes in unusual places. Ninety per cent of women prefer white or black. That's a lot of unused underwear sitting at the back of drawers and a lot of disappointed women. I should think there's an advertising opportunity for you in there somewhere.'

'I'll bear it in mind.'

'Of course,' she added conversationally, 'for five per cent of women it's irrelevant anyway.'

'Why?'

'Because they don't wear any underwear at all.'

'Five per cent?'

Zoe nodded. 'Five per cent.' Surely it had to be about that?

'Draughty,' he murmured, still resolutely staring out of the window.

'It can be,' she said, and with a little wiggle deliberately pulled the hem of her dress down.

That got his attention. And that of the taxi driver if the spluttered cough that came from the front seat was anything to go by.

In the ensuing thundering silence she heard Dan inhale slowly, deeply, as if bracing himself, and then watched as he slowly twisted round, his eyes landing on her thighs before travelling up the length of her and finally meeting her own.

And then it was her turn to draw in a sharp breath because the fierce hunger in his expression, the desire blazing in the depths of his eyes and the rigid tension radiating off his body was just about rendering her boneless. Oh, he wasn't regretting his decision, she thought dazedly. He wasn't regretting it at all.

'You'll catch your death,' he said, his eyes glittering dangerously and his face all dark and tight.

'Want to warm me up?' she suggested, although he was doing a pretty good job of that with just his gaze.

'Very much so.'

'Then what are you waiting for?'

Dan cast a quick glance at the taxi driver before turning back to her and practically pinning her to the seat with the intensity of his gaze. 'Privacy.'

She pouted. 'Party pooper.'

He gave her a glimmer of a smile. 'Not at all,' he said. 'We're here.'

So they were, thought Zoe, wrenching her eyes from his and seeing they were pulling up outside a house at one end of a fine Georgian terrace. And a good thing it was too because despite her aversion to exhibitionism she wasn't sure she could stop herself from touching him for much longer.

While Dan paid the driver she got out, her limbs feeling so loose and wobbly that she had to clutch onto the side of the taxi in order not to stumble. Then he grabbed her hand and strode across the pavement and up the three steps to the front door. He unlocked the door and ushered her inside and closed it behind them, instantly blocking out the rumbling of the city and the chill of the night and cocooning them in the warm quiet shadows of the hall.

She watched him turn the key in the lock, her pulse racing and her breath becoming all shallow and shaky. He slowly turned to her and for a moment they just stared at each other and then it was as if they were springs that had been held apart and suddenly let go.

As he lunged for her Zoe dropped her handbag and lurched forwards. He pulled her into his arms and hauled her up against him and she wound her arms around his neck and lifted her head at the same time as he lowered his. His lips crashed down onto hers and his tongue slid into her mouth and deep inside she felt desire flood through her like a great rush of water breaking through a dam wall.

Managing to slip her coat off with one hand, Dan slid his other hand up and into her hair and angled her head, and as he deepened the kiss Zoe melted into him. She moaned and shivered at the feel of his erection against her stomach. She arched her back and pressed herself even closer and with a soft groan Dan twisted her round, pushing her up against the front door and pinning her body to it with his hips.

He planted his hands either side of her head and then he tore his mouth away from hers. She gasped for breath, her heart thundering so hard she feared it might leap from her chest, and was just about to protest about the absence of his mouth when his lips connected with her jaw, trailed along to her ear and then down, and any protest she'd had died in her throat.

'What the hell was all that about?' he muttered against her neck.

What with the way her skin was burning and her head swimming Zoe could barely think let alone speak. 'What was what all about?' she said hoarsely, threading her fingers through his hair, closing her eyes and tipping her head back to give him better access to her throat.

'Road markings.'

'A distraction,' she managed and gasped as he gently nipped the skin covering her collarbone.

She felt his mouth curve into a smile against the pulse at the base of her neck. 'I was going for the studiously ignoring you approach.'

'And there was me thinking you just weren't all that interested in traffic planning.'

'I was more interested in the underwear part,' he said, lifting his head and staring down at her. 'Or rather the lack of it. Now *that's* a fascinating subject. Five per cent, did you say?'

Zoe blushed. 'I might have been a little sketchy on the percentages.'

'And you, a statistician? I'm appalled.'

'Didn't you know eighty-six per cent of statistics are made up?'

'I thought it was forty-two.'

'No, it's definitely sixty-seven.'

He bent his head and murmured into her ear, 'Tell me more about this absence of underwear. In your particular experience.'

Zoe shivered as the vibration of his voice and the warmth of his breath curled all the way through her. 'I might have been a bit misleading on that front, too.'

'Oh dear, twice in one night?'

'I wanted to get your undivided attention.'

'You got it. You have it.'

'I know.'

Dan moved his hands to her waist and her breath hitched in her throat. 'Perhaps I'd better check, though, just to see whether there's any "might" about it.'

'You know, you're full of good ideas.'

He drew back a little and smiled down at her. 'I've barely even started.'

'Well, I'm not going anywhere.'

'No,' he said, his eyes burning into hers, the look in them making her heart thump even more crazily. 'You aren't.'

He slid his hands up her ribcage, skimming the undersides of her breasts as he searched for the zip of her dress and Zoe shivered.

'Cold?' he murmured, finding the tab at the side and beginning to tug it down, so slowly that at first her dress did nothing but gape a little.

'Boiling.'

He pulled the zip further, all the way down until it stopped and her dress just sort of fell apart, slithering down her body and pooling at her feet.

'Better?' he asked.

'Not really.' Not when she was standing there in nothing more than a white lacy strapless push-up bra, matching knickers, nude hold-ups and shoes, with only a pearl choker for decoration, and his eyes were roaming all over her with a hunger that robbed her of breath.

'Not one of the five per cent, then.'

Zoe swallowed. 'Disappointed?'

'Disappointed is not the word that springs to mind.'

'What word does?'

'Stunning.'

'That one will do.'

As Dan resumed his perusal of her he appeared to descend into speechlessness and immobility and Zoe took the opportunity to balance things up a bit on the sartorial front.

Pushing his coat and then his jacket off his shoulders and letting them fall to join her dress on the floor, she went to work on the buttons of his shirt. Her hands were shaking so much it took twice as long as she reckoned it should have but, God, was it a task worth pursuing because when she parted the two panels of cotton and caught her first glimpse of his chest she realised that what was in front of her was a body that Michelangelo would have wept buckets of awe over.

There wasn't an over-pumped muscle in sight, just an expanse of tanned skin brushed with a smattering of hair that stretched over taut flesh and tapered down over the hint of a six-pack.

Unable to hold back, she put her hands on him and when she felt him tremble beneath her palms a sense of power and amazement that she could do this to a man like him surged up inside her and addled her brain.

In mouth-watering fascination she watched her hands trail down to the fastening of his trousers as if acting entirely of their own accord. Her fingers undid the button and slid down the zip and then slipped inside to feel the hot hard length of him.

At the thought of him pushing into her, she started to ache and throb with such desire, such desperation, that she actually moaned as she curled her hand around him and began to stroke it up and down.

Dan snapped out of his rigid immobility and galvanised into action. 'Bedroom,' he said, wrapping a hand around her wrist and stopping what she was doing.

'No,' she muttered, thinking that if she didn't get him inside her right now she might just expire right here on the floor of the hall.

'Yes.'

'Why?'

'Condoms.'

Good point. 'Lead the way.'

As he pushed his trousers down and stepped out of them Zoe kicked off her shoes, then put her hand into the one he held out and followed him up the stairs that were hard to negotiate given her legs had turned to jelly. He led her into his room, flicked a switch that bathed the room in soft pale yellow light and kicked the door shut.

Zoe didn't have the chance to look round, or even check out the bed, because her eyes locked with his and all she could see was him. Then he was walking her backwards until the backs of her knees hit something hard and he was giving her a gentle push so she fell back on the bed.

Then she found she couldn't have checked out his furnishings even if she'd wanted to because Dan was stripping what little remained of his clothing, rummaging around in a drawer and then slipping on a condom and as it struck her she was about to have out-of-this-world sex her mouth went dry and her head went all foggy.

Dan lowered himself over her and settled his mouth on hers and all she could think about was how delicious kissing him was. How wickedly clever he was. He knew exactly how to make her whimper, how to make her pant and moan and beg simply by concentrating on her mouth, her lips and her tongue.

By the time he rolled onto his back, taking her with him so that she sprawled on top of him, Zoe was a rioting mass of sensation inside. Every nerve ending she possessed was quivering and jumping and desperate for more.

He unclipped her bra and she wriggled as he tugged it from between them. Then while she revelled in the friction of his hair against her breasts he slid his hands down her back and over her bottom, slipping his fingers beneath her knickers and easing them down. Then he rolled her back over so he could remove them altogether. Which he did. Achingly slowly. Sliding them over her hips and down her legs, stroking over her skin as he did so. He took the same care with her hold-ups and by the time he was finished all Zoe could think was that she was about to explode with need.

She couldn't stand another second of the torture. Of the torment. Instinct took over. Batting Dan's hands out of the way, she reared up and he automatically sat back on his heels. Which was just perfect for what she wanted. Before he could even begin to look surprised, she straddled his hips. She wrapped one arm around his neck and took his erection in the other hand and with a deep groan sank herself onto him.

She locked her legs around his back and tucked her head into the nook where his neck met his shoulders, delirious for a moment just to feel him buried deep, stretching her, filling her and throbbing inside her.

Dan went rigidly still. He was tense and his jaw was tight and she wasn't sure if it was because he didn't trust himself to stay in control or whether he was in shock at the boldness of her move. Having no intention whatsoever of asking, Zoe decided to just carry on as she wanted and see what happened. So she kissed her way up his neck. She found his mouth and slid her tongue between his lips, tilted her hips and felt him lodge even deeper.

And then something clearly snapped inside him because he clamped one hand to the back of her head, the other against her lower back and he rocked her back. Looming over her, his eyes glittering dark and hot and his muscles strained, he began to move.

And with all that power and strength above her, being used with such perfectly deadly intent, Zoe felt herself begin to unravel. Her insides buckled and melted and as she felt a wave of pleasure begin to roll through her her breath came faster, shallower. Beginning to pant and moan and too far gone to even care that she might be begging, she gripped Dan's arms and clung on for dear life as the wave gathered strength and rushed towards her.

His thrusts became harder, deeper, faster and the frown on his face deepened and then that wave hit and with a sharp cry she shattered, convulsing over and over again around him as the pleasure splintered inside her.

And then he lowered himself down to her, held her face and kissed her hard and fiercely as he buried himself deep and pulsated into her.

For quite a while the only noise filling the room was the sound of their breathing, at first loud, ragged and harsh, then gradually quietening and evening out.

'Well, that certainly beats the ski resort in Italy,' said Zoe once she'd recovered her voice and her brain was back in its usual place.

Dan rolled off her and fell back. 'It certainly beats my expectations.'

She propped herself up on an elbow and looked down at him quizzically. 'You had expectations?'

'Many.'

'Since when?'

'Since last night when I dreamed about you.'

That sounded nice. 'What was I doing?'

'This,' he said with a wicked smile. 'With variations on the theme.'

'And I was good?'

'Very good.'

Zoe smiled and stretched and then flopped back against the pillows. '*I* dreamed about broccoli.'

A look of bemusement passed across his face. 'Broccoli?'

She nodded. 'A great towering spear of the stuff was

marching towards me like some sort of giant mutated tree, chanting "eat me". I guess I'm a little low on iron.'

A little low on appropriateness as well, it belatedly struck her, because she'd just had the out-of-this-world sex she'd been hoping for and all she could talk about was the nutritional benefit of broccoli? Was there really no hope for her?

Groaning, Zoe flapped a hand and then clapped it over her eyes, 'Oh, God, ignore me.'

She heard him laugh softly. 'Impossible.'

'If you want to send me home now I wouldn't blame you in the slightest.'

'I don't want to send you home now.'

Zoe gingerly removed her hand to glance at him, just in case she was imagining the sincerity in his voice. 'You don't?'

'No.'

'Oh, good.'

'In fact, I'm thinking you should stay the night.'

A wave of warmth rolled over her and she felt a great goofy smile begin to spread across her face. 'And I'm thinking I'd like that.'

CHAPTER EIGHT

WHAT A NIGHT, thought Zoe, gradually coming to and stretching beneath the warm cosy duvet while her brain caught up with her body in the waking-up stakes. And what a morning…

Blinking away the remnants of sleep and rubbing her eyes, she smiled a smile that she was glad no one could see because she was sure it was wide and satisfied and way too smug.

She'd been one hundred per cent right in thinking that sex with Dan would be of the stupendous kind. It had surpassed all her wildest dreams and her dreams had been pretty wild. And even though she didn't have much to compare it with she was pretty sure that most people didn't have multiple orgasms all through the night or moan and groan so much that their throat wound up sore. As for her body, well, she ached in places she hadn't known existed. She'd discovered muscles she didn't think she'd ever used and she'd learned that she was more supple than she'd ever imagined.

'Good morning,' muttered a rough voice from beside her and Zoe pulled down the duvet to look at the cause of her aches, her lethargy and her bonelessness.

'Is it?' she mumbled. 'Morning, I mean.'

Dan twisted back around, all those fabulous muscles

flexing and pulling, picked his watch up off the bedside table and squinted at it. 'Just about. It's half past eleven.'

'Heavens, I haven't slept beyond seven in years,' she said with a yawn, 'but then I don't normally have a night like the one I've just had.'

He put his watch back down and rolled over to face her once again. 'How are you feeling?'

She grinned. 'Fabulous. Exhausted. Achy.'

'Me too.'

He propped himself up, then leaned over and bent down to kiss her, and any brief panic about morning breath disappeared beneath a surge of desire. The kiss was lazy and long, and wiped out the aches faster than any hot bath. By the time he lifted his head, Zoe was so hot she was surprised she hadn't melted.

'So what happens now?' she asked breathlessly, kind of hoping he wasn't going to tell her it was time to go home as she wasn't sure she was able to walk.

'I could make you coffee,' he said with the glimmer of a smile.

'That sounds nice,' she said. 'And then?'

'Brunch?'

She gave him an exasperated look and batted him on the arm. 'Ouch,' he said mildly.

'Wimp,' she said, grinning up at him. 'What I'm trying to ask, as you're well aware, is do you want to do this again?'

'What do you think?' he asked, taking her in his arms and rolling her on top of him so she could feel exactly how keen he was to do it again.

Zoe pushed herself up and off him before the desire he whipped up inside her could suck her under again, taking a handful of duvet with her as she sat back on the bed. 'I don't mean now,' she said, clutching the duvet to her chest as if it might provide some sort of defence against his addictiveness. 'I mean another time.'

'Sounds good to me,' he said, his smile fading, and his expression turned serious as he too levered himself up. 'But there's something you should know.'

At the gravity of his tone Zoe felt herself pale and her heart dropped. Oh dear, this didn't sound good. He'd told her that he wasn't married and he didn't have a girlfriend, so what could it be? Was he ill? Not who he said he was? Did he have a criminal record?

'What is it?' she asked, and braced herself.

'I have a three-date-only rule.'

Huh? Zoe blinked, wondering for a moment if she'd misheard. 'A what?'

'I only ever have a maximum of three dates—and discreet ones at that—with any one woman.'

That was what she thought he'd said. 'Why?'

He rubbed a hand along his jaw. 'I can't risk another kiss-and-tell.'

Zoe bristled. 'I've no interest in kissing and telling.'

'I'm sure you don't,' he said so smoothly it sounded like a line he'd used quite a few times before. 'But that's the rule.'

'Is it negotiable?'

'No.'

She bit her lip. 'I see.'

'If you don't like it I wouldn't blame you.'

She wasn't sure what she thought of it but as she turned it over in her mind Zoe supposed she couldn't blame him for being wary. Although the way he was only mentioning it now, when she was already reeled in, did seem slightly underhand. 'Bit late to bring up rules now, don't you think?'

Dan frowned. 'Yes, I'm sorry. I should have mentioned it last night. But I wasn't thinking entirely straight, not that that's any excuse.'

Zoe grinned. 'It's fine. I'm flattered I had you so be-fuddled. Anyway, why three?'

'What?'

'Well, why not two dates, or four, or something? Why three?'

'I don't know.' He shrugged, but Zoe didn't entirely trust his air of ignorance. Not when to her it seemed pretty obvious.

'Let me guess,' she said, tapping her fingers against her mouth for a moment. 'A three-date limit means there's no need for the exchange of too much personal information, no need for intimate chit-chat or any of those pesky strings that come with relationships, yet the chances of sex are pretty good.'

'You make it sound grubby,' he said, although she noticed he didn't deny it.

'I don't think it's anything. It's your policy, not mine. Does it work?'

He shot her a rueful smile. 'Not all that well, to be honest.'

'You mean there aren't that many women after nothing more than a one-night stand with you?' She grinned. 'You amaze me.'

'Why? Aren't you one of them?'

Hmm. The man was perceptive, she'd give him that. 'You have a point, although this is strictly a one-off. But if you're so worried about a kiss-and-tell why not just get them to sign a confidentiality agreement?'

He stared at her for a moment as if the idea of it had never crossed his mind. 'Would *you* do that?'

'Of course, although I doubt anyone would seriously believe you and I would be involved anyway.'

'Why not?'

'Because you're practically a god,' she said, waving a

hand in his direction and then in hers, 'and I'm…well… not much of a goddess.'

'I don't know about that,' said Dan dryly. 'Some of the things you did last night were pretty divine.'

'Yes, well, you were very encouraging.'

Snapshots of what they'd done together last night flitted into her head, and his too she thought, judging by the long seconds of silence that followed.

'Did you actually see the article about us?' he asked eventually, yanking her out of her very lovely memories and making her pale with his words.

'Us?' she echoed.

Reaching over, Dan fished for his phone, messed about with it for a bit, then turned the screen round and handed it to her. 'Have a look at this.'

Taking the phone from him, Zoe began to read, her heart sinking with every word. First there was the news about their engagement, which was melodramatic and sensationalised and about as far from the rather unromantic truth as it was possible to be. Following that was a paragraph about her, which managed to make her sound dry, boring and totally insignificant. And then came reams and reams about Dan, about his advertising brilliance, his eligibility and the women he'd been seen with, of which there were many, all high-profile.

'I see,' she said when she'd finished it. 'No wonder you had to deny it.'

'I didn't have a choice.'

She handed the phone back to him. 'Of course you didn't. I mean, really? Why would anyone think you were ever engaged to me for real? The gorgeous hotshot Casanova and the dull, plain statistician? Hah. I don't think so.'

'What? No. That wasn't what I meant.' He looked at her closely and then frowned. 'But God, they really did a number on you, didn't they?' he said softly.

She glanced away. 'Who did?'

'The bullies.'

'I don't know what you mean.'

'You know exactly what I mean.'

She shrugged. 'Maybe they did.'

'Just maybe?' he asked.

'OK, so I have a couple of self-esteem issues. But it's nothing I can't deal with.'

'If you say so.'

'I do.'

'What I don't get, though,' said Dan, flopping back on the pillows and linking his hands behind his head, 'is why they targeted *you*?'

Momentarily distracted by the sight of him lying there, his broad shoulders looking even broader with his arms up like that, his entire chest on display for her, Zoe swallowed hard and dragged her eyes away from his muscles and up to his face, the better to concentrate. 'Why wouldn't they?' she murmured.

'You don't seem the type to take it.'

'You've only known me for forty-eight hours. I've been around for a whole thirty-two years.'

'Tell me more.'

Zoe frowned. 'Why? Isn't this exactly the sort of personal stuff your three-date rule is designed to avoid?'

'I'd simply like to be able to put Thursday night into perspective, that's all.'

Maybe she did owe him that much, she supposed, especially since he'd helped her out so magnificently. 'OK, well, I guess I never really fitted in.'

'At school?'

'Anywhere. Right from when I was little I never got what made people gel.' She sighed softly. 'At primary school everyone was always huddled in little groups and I could never work out what they were talking about. There they were playing make believe and all I could think was why? What was the point? So I just stood there hanging around on the sidelines, not joining in, not being invited to birthday parties and not going on play dates.'

'And it bothered you?'

'A bit, but mainly because I couldn't work out what to do about it.'

'What happened when you got to secondary school?'

She winced. 'Oh, well, things got a lot worse obviously.'

'Why obviously?'

'Because what had been instinct became deliberate.' She shook her head and shot him a look. 'Teenage girls in a pack on a mission? You do *not* want to be in their sights.'

'I can't begin to imagine,' he muttered with a frown.

'I was rubbish at acting and music and sport, which was all any of the girls really cared about when it came to the curriculum, but I did have an affinity for numbers. I was kind of obsessed with them and it made me stand out.' She shrugged. 'People thought I was weird.'

'I don't.'

Zoe gave him a wry smile. 'No, but you're not a teenage girl who thinks studying is square and instead is obsessed with boys, iridescent make-up and snogging.'

His gaze dipped to her mouth and his eyes darkened. 'I quite like the snogging part.'

'So do I. Now. But then I couldn't care less about it. Anyway, weirdness wasn't a trait that was celebrated at St Catherine's, so really I didn't stand a chance.'

'How bad did it get?'

She shrugged. 'Pretty bad.'

'Did you ever do anything about it?'

'Once. When I saw red and lashed out at random. Unfortunately I caught Samantha on the chin and she fell and got concussion.'

'Did she report it?'

Zoe shook her head. 'And have me tell everyone why I'd done it? Oh no. She was far cleverer than that. She force-fed me half a bottle of ouzo that she'd smuggled in after a summer holiday in Greece and got me suspended instead.' She sighed. 'I swear I can still taste the stuff sometimes.' Then she shot him a small smile. 'But on the bright side at least YouTube wasn't around then.'

'I wish I'd known all this on Thursday night,' he muttered.

'Why?'

'I'd have been far less…restrained.'

Zoe felt warmth steal through her and her heart squeezed at the fierce look blazing in the depths of his eyes. 'The bullying might not have done much for my self-esteem, but, God, you do.'

'Agree to the three-date rule and I'll do my best to boost it as much as I can.'

She stared at him. Three dates only. Hmm. She certainly wanted some more of that lovely sex, but could she really give it up in three dates' time as she'd undoubtedly have to? That might be tough. On the other hand walking away now and not having any more of the lovely sex did seem a bit like cutting off her nose to spite her face.

So the two roads open to her were fabulous sex for a short time or no sex at all. It was a no-brainer.

'Sounds good to me,' she said, renewed desire beginning to seep through her and tangle with hunger.

'Great. How about tonight for date number one?'

'Doesn't last night count?'

'Seeing as how I omitted to mention the rule, I don't think it should, do you?'

'A good point,' she said graciously. 'And a fair one.'

'So, tonight?'

'I can do tonight.'

'Really?' he said looking at her quizzically. 'Are you

sure you aren't impossibly busy for the next week but perhaps could fit me in on Thursday between six and seven?'

'I don't play those kinds of games.'

'Well, what kinds of games do you play?' he asked, a light suddenly shining in his eyes.

'Feed me first and then I'll show you.'

Oddly enough, the end of date number three, a week later, came round far too quickly for Dan's liking.

He'd implemented the rule to prevent the need for intimacy and to avoid the disclosure of any personal information that might be of interest to the paper-reading public, which up to now had worked rather too well, as—as Zoe had so perceptively pointed out—not many of the women who expressed an interest in him and vice versa were happy with his conditions. But somehow with Zoe sex on its own didn't seem to be enough.

He wanted to know more about her. A lot more. The taster she'd given him when he'd asked her about the effect the bullying had had on her had left him wondering what she felt about and how she dealt with other things, like her family, her business, her friends. He wanted to know what she thought about politics, current affairs, whether she had any hobbies. But as he'd been so bloody pig-headed about the rule in the first place he'd hardly been able to break it and ask her.

However, now they were coming to the end of it, he was thinking that if Zoe were amenable and if they agreed to keep things low-key perhaps they could renegotiate the deal.

It would require something of a leap of faith because even though what he was about to suggest wouldn't expose him to the possibility of a kiss-and-tell, it would leave him vulnerable nonetheless. But then what was he going to do?

Stick to his guns and be alone for ever? That sounded even less appealing.

'So I guess this is it, then,' said Zoe, sitting on the edge of the bed all dressed and ready to leave, her expression unfathomable.

'It doesn't have to be.'

Her eyebrows lifted. 'No?'

Dan took a deep breath and hoped to God he wasn't making a colossal mistake. 'What would you say to signing that confidentiality agreement you mentioned?'

Well, that was a suggestion she'd never anticipated, Zoe thought, staring at Dan in surprise as he watched her closely. He'd been so intractable about the three-date thing that she'd worked herself up to leaving without a backward glance and burying the week somewhere deep in her memory, but not so far that she couldn't visit and indulge herself from time to time.

But now he'd thrown a curve ball, one that appealed more than it should, which meant she was going to have to have a rethink.

'Why?' she asked, mainly to give herself some time to do just that.

'Because I don't want this to be over.' He paused for a second, then asked, 'Do you?'

'I don't know.'

Which was the truth. The last three dates had been great, light on small talk, heavy on sex, which had suited her perfectly because it had meant that while she'd been having a lot of fun he hadn't asked any more probing and potentially humiliation-inducing questions about her past and she hadn't had to answer. It had also meant they hadn't gone out and therefore hadn't been anywhere where the press might express an interest.

If she started dating him properly, however, as he seemed

to be implying he wanted, then that would change. They'd inevitably go out from time to time, and the press would undoubtedly take an interest. Depending on how long things lasted, they might even dig around for stuff about her. They might talk to Samantha and her pals, which wouldn't be pretty. Even worse, her appearance would be scrutinised and would inevitably be criticised. She knew how stuff like this worked. Sort of. And would she be able to handle it? She wasn't sure.

But on the other hand, now she was being presented with the offer of an extension to their mini-fling, she was wavering. She'd finally got round to Googling him and, although she'd tried not to be too interested in what she read by telling herself that there was no point in thinking of questions she'd never be able to ask, she couldn't deny that her appetite to learn more about him had been whetted.

And really if anything did make its way into the papers would it really be such a big deal? She hardly ever read the things anyway.

'Would it still be just about the sex?' she asked, teetering on the tipping point.

He arched an eyebrow. 'I don't see how it could be, do you?'

At the thought she might be on the brink of a real relationship with a man like Dan her pulse began to race. 'Could we be discreet?'

He grinned. 'I can't believe you have to ask when you know how in favour of discretion I am.'

'OK,' she said, feeling a thrill ripple through her as over the edge she went, 'then why not?'

CHAPTER NINE

FOUR WEEKS LATER, and Zoe could hardly believe that at one point she'd ever seriously contemplated not wanting to go out with Dan.

She must have been nuts, she thought, pushing through the revolving door at the entrance of her office and stepping out onto the street, because quite honestly these last few weeks had been some of the best of her life. Better than her A-level fortnight, better than her finals and better even than her viva, which was saying something.

And it wasn't just the sex, although that was pretty high up there on her list of things to be pleased about. It was the conversation too, the exchange of personal information that neither of them had ever intended to do.

Tangled in sheets and basking in the aftermath of explosive passion, they'd conversationally meandered through topics such as siblings, parents and careers, and he hadn't once tried to deflect her questions the way she'd half expected him to.

She'd told him about her love of numbers, the black and white nature of them and their fail-safe reliability, and he'd confessed to the thrill he still got when everything came together to create a great advertising campaign and his regret that he no longer had the time to do much on the creative side. She'd talked about her future plans for her business and he'd mentioned his intention to expand his operations by putting in an offer for the US agency that was up for sale.

She'd touched on her sister and her disaster of a marriage, and he'd told her about Celia and the devastating effect their parents' divorce had had on her.

She'd told him more about her school years and he'd told her about the traumatic time he'd had during his, when his parents had been at the height of their arguing and things had been tough for a while.

The only thing they didn't talk about was their relationship and where it was going, but that was fine with Zoe because she wasn't sure where she wanted them to be going.

At the moment, for her at least, things were going just great. Dan didn't seem to be put off either by her idiosyncrasies or her insecurities; on the contrary he seemed respectively fascinated by and supportive of them, and if she'd been more into the arts than the sciences she'd have said she was blossoming beneath all the attention he showered her with.

As agreed they'd kept a low profile, staying in more than they'd been out, and that suited Zoe just fine too because despite her self-assurances to the contrary she *had* been worrying a bit about the possibility of press intrusion and what might be said about her.

And yes, a couple of photos of them had popped up on the Internet and in the papers, with a comment or two that she didn't much care for, but generally she didn't warrant much interest. She wasn't a glamorous actress, after all— and of course she'd Googled Jasmine Thomas even though she'd immediately wished she hadn't because the woman was absolutely gorgeous—and she wasn't famous or newsworthy or anything. She was just someone who was having fun. A lot of it.

And with any luck she'd be having some more of it tonight, she thought, smiling to herself as she gripped onto the strap of her handbag and weaved her way through the crowds towards the tube station.

Dan was off to the States tomorrow to go and check up on the company he was planning to buy, and she was cooking him a farewell dinner, which involved hours of preparation, lots of expensive ingredients and going home early for a bit of pampering.

She was trying not to think about how much she was going to miss him, but that was proving to be nigh on impossible because she feared she was going to miss him hugely. She'd got used to his calls, his emails, the hot hard kiss he always gave her whenever they met up that was better than any hello, even the light snoring he swore he didn't do. The calls and emails she guessed she'd still get, but the kisses and the snoring she'd pine for terribly.

The disproportionate strength of her reaction to the thought of not having him around for what was only a week would have made her stop and wonder if she hadn't been feeling so jittery and tense and sick.

Of course the nerves and the edginess and the nausea churning through her could well be PMT, she thought, swearing beneath her breath when someone bumped into her, because she always felt a bit tense and snappish a day or two before her period.

Not usually nauseous though, but then seeing as she'd been on something of an emotional roller coaster ever since she'd met Dan, and hadn't eaten all day in anticipation of this evening's feast, perhaps nausea was only to be expected.

Or was it something else?

Zoe stopped dead, right there in the middle of the street with people streaming round her on their way home, the bottom falling out of her stomach and the world around her going fuzzy.

Hang on.

She and Dan had been sleeping with each other, for what, a month now, and she hadn't had a period. Over a month, actually, she thought, her heart hammering and her head pounding as she calculated the dates.

She was late. Way late. Which didn't look good.

Oh, *God*.

A film of sweat broke out all over her body and her clothes suddenly felt tight, constricting. Her head swam and her legs went all weak and shaky because a pregnancy had never featured in any part of her plan to have fun. She didn't think it featured anywhere in Dan's either, although they'd never talked about stuff like that. Hell, they barely talked about their plans beyond a week in advance, but a man who generally didn't proceed beyond three dates wasn't likely to welcome the lifetime commitment of a child.

What she and Dan were having was nothing more than a fling. He'd never indicated that he was interested in anything else and now she came to think about it every time he'd told her something personal he'd subtly managed to work in a reference to the confidentiality agreement she'd signed. He clearly kept it at the forefront of his mind, whether consciously or subconsciously, and whatever way she looked at it the fact was it wasn't a sign of someone who was about to throw himself into a full-blown strings-and-everything relationship. Nor was the fact she hadn't met any of his family or friends and he hadn't expressed any interest in meeting hers.

So if she *was* pregnant then what would she do? Would she get rid of it? Would she keep it? If she did keep it then how would she cope when she wasn't sure she even liked children? Financially, she was fine of course, but emotionally, well, who knew where she was with that?

And God, what if the press were to find out? she thought, beginning to hyperventilate as random thoughts whipped round her head. They'd have a field day and Dan would be

furious and he'd think she'd done it on purpose to trap him
or something and it would all be her fault, even though of
course it wasn't, and—

Telling herself she had to calm down before she passed
out on the pavement, Zoe drew in a deep steadying breath
and then let it out as slowly as she could.

She had to stop and think about this logically and rationally because maybe, on the other hand, there wasn't anything to worry about. She'd never been all that regular, and,
what with the stress of work lately and the high she'd been
riding with Dan, perhaps her cycle was merely struggling
to cope. And they had been so very careful.

Either way, she thought, summoning strength to her
limbs and changing course for the pharmacy across the
road, the minute she got home she'd better do a test because she wasn't sure she could cope with the uncertainty.

Half an hour later, Zoe was sitting on the edge of the
bath at home, staring at the test, and as only one little line
showed up and relief flooded through her she thought, Well,
thank *God* for that.

How he'd ever thought three dates with Zoe would be
enough he'd never know, thought Dan, staring up at the
ceiling and listening to the soft sounds of her breathing
next to him.

He'd enjoyed these past few weeks far more than he'd
ever imagined, and to his amazement he was going to miss
her while he was away because so far things had been going
pretty much perfectly.

Quite apart from their explosive compatibility in bed,
he enjoyed her company out of it too. She was intelligent—
way more intelligent than he was, he'd discovered when
he'd once jokingly asked her what her IQ was—and funny,
usually unintentionally.

As they'd talked he'd found her increasingly fascinating. The contrast between her uber-confident professional side and her less confident personal side was intriguing and something he was, oddly enough, enjoying dissecting.

He was beginning to realise that Zoe was different from the women he generally came across. She didn't cling and she didn't demand, and refreshingly she seemed perfectly happy with the way things were going.

She might roll her eyes whenever he casually dropped the confidentiality agreement into conversation but she hadn't once asked him to tear it up, and, even though he'd never implemented it before so he didn't have anyone to compare her with, he suspected that not everyone would have agreed to sign such a thing without some kind of complaint or a condition perhaps that they revise it at a later date.

So Zoe was pretty much everything he wanted in a woman, and that was undoubtedly why even though he was only going for a week the idea of coming back to her was surprisingly reassuring.

Now that he thought about it, actually, he wouldn't mind if she were always there when he came back from somewhere. For a while longer, at least.

Contrary to popular belief he'd never had a problem with the concept of commitment. Despite his parents' disaster of a marriage and nightmare of a divorce he didn't even have much of a problem with marriage either, at least not in the abstract. It was just that it seemed to him that commitment required trust, and, as his ability to do that had been well and truly shot to pieces by first Natalie, finally Jasmine and quite a few other women in between, it wasn't an issue that had ever cropped up.

But maybe things were changing. Maybe *he* was changing, because lately he'd been thinking he wouldn't really mind if Zoe's wash bag were to appear in his bathroom. He wouldn't mind leaving a toothbrush in hers.

Dan rubbed a hand over his face and frowned into the darkness as he wondered what it meant. Was he falling for her? It didn't seem beyond the realms of possibility, but if he was then what was he going to do about it? Love, if it should ever come to that, hadn't exactly worked out well for him the last time he'd tried it. In fact it had worked out abysmally. When his relationship with Natalie had imploded he'd gone so completely off the rails that he'd narrowly avoided jail and he wasn't exactly keen for it to happen again.

As his mouth filled with a sudden bitter taste Dan eased himself off the bed and crept into the en suite bathroom in search of water.

He reached for a glass. He turned on the tap, filled the glass and looked up.

And then he saw it. The pregnancy test box, sitting there on the shelf, and everything around it faded away and all thoughts of how he might or might not feel about Zoe and what he would or wouldn't do about it shot clean from his head.

With his heart thumping even harder and his fingers trembling even more he put down the glass and picked up the box. Gave it a shake. It was empty. He glanced down at the bin and now a trickle of sweat began to make its way down his spine. He lifted the lid gingerly. Closed his eyes and took a deep breath and then looked. But that was empty too.

And then his head began to pound as questions suddenly started flying around inside. Was she or wasn't she? Now he thought about it she hadn't had her period since she'd known him, and that had been, what, five weeks? That didn't sound good. So if she was, how would he feel about it? If she wasn't, how would he feel? When had she done the test? When was she planning on telling him? *Was* she planning on telling him?

Despite the warm cosiness of the bathroom Dan went ice-cold as memories of another time, another woman, another pregnancy slammed into his head. As his knees threatened to give way he planted both hands on the edge of the basin tightly.

On some dim and distant level he knew he wasn't thinking about this rationally, that things were different this time, that Zoe wasn't Natalie and he wasn't twenty-five, but this awareness was slipping further and further away with every second that the feeling he'd lost his grip on something he'd thought he could control intensified.

His head went fuzzy and his vision blurred and he thought he might be about to pass out.

And that brought him up sharp. Taking a deep shuddery breath, Dan gave himself a shake and pulled himself together. He shook his head and straightened. Shoved his hands through his hair and drank that glass of water and then he felt slightly better.

But the questions and the memories were still ricocheting round his head, making him feel weak. He needed perspective. He needed time and he needed space to work things out and tomorrow wasn't soon enough. He need it all right now.

Almost stumbling back into the bedroom, Dan picked up his clothes and somehow managed to get them on.

'What are you doing?' Zoe murmured sleepily and then stretched, and he gritted his teeth against the sudden fierce temptation to climb back into bed with her and postpone thinking about it all until tomorrow.

'I have to go,' he muttered.

She rubbed her eyes and pushed a hand through her hair. 'Now?'

'Early flight.'

'I thought you weren't leaving until the evening.'

'Change of plan.'

'Oh, OK,' she said with a slow sexy smile that only made him more confused. 'Have a good trip.'

Right. That was it. Zoe had had enough.

Dan had been back from the States for a week, but he might as well have stayed there because while physically he'd returned he certainly wasn't here in spirit. Ever since he'd got back he'd been distant and cool, and it was as perplexing as it was frustrating.

Especially when she'd spent that entire week missing him so much. Her period had arrived the day after she'd done the test, as if doing it had given it permission or something, and so not only had she had to deal with missing him, she'd also had to put up with cramps and moodiness. The only thing that had kept her going had been the thought she'd soon be seeing him, and she'd been *so* looking forward to it.

But although she and Dan had caught up a few times since he'd been back, every single moment she'd spent with him she'd had the feeling that something wasn't quite right.

From time to time she'd look at him and find him watching her, his eyes dark and inscrutable, his face unreadable. She'd had the disturbing feeling he was assessing her. Evaluating her every move, from what she ate and drank to the way she spoke and behaved. And waiting, although for what she had no idea.

It was weird. It was more than weird, actually, she thought, following him into his house and mentally revisiting the dinner out that they'd just had, which had been a strangely uncomfortable and stressful couple of hours. He'd been so odd and aloof this evening that she knew she'd wildly overcompensated, laughing a little too loudly, smiling a little too brightly and talking a little too fast.

His attitude was horrible, and made her feel on edge and confused. Whatever it was that was bothering him she wanted to know, because frankly she'd had enough of it. So what if it meant conflict? So what if it meant awkwardness? She had to do *something*.

Dan wasn't sure how much more of this awful waiting—and hoping—he could take. Dinner earlier had been hellish. Zoe had been chatting and laughing and talking about God knew what and all he'd been able to think was, should she be drinking that gimlet? Should she be eating those prawns?

He was clinging onto his sanity and his control by his fingertips and it was agony. His perspective was no clearer than it had been the night everything had begun to implode. If anything, it was even more clouded, and now he was struggling to see the wood for the trees.

The last couple of weeks had been tough, and not just because he'd had a hectic week in America and then crippling jet lag. He'd tried to keep reminding himself what he'd told himself in the bathroom: that Zoe wasn't Natalie and that if there was anything to tell she'd tell him. But it kept being drowned out by the thought, the fear, that history could well be repeating itself, and he didn't know how to handle any of it.

'Dan?' said Zoe, and at the cool firm note in her voice he turned around.

'What?'

'We need to talk.'

Thank God. Finally. 'You're right,' he said, as the thought that everything might turn out OK after all entered his head. 'We do.'

'I'm glad you think so.'

'Shall we sit down?'

'I think we might need to.'

They walked into the kitchen where Dan pulled out a chair for Zoe to sit down and then took the one opposite.

For a moment they just stared at each other as if waiting for the other to start, and then he couldn't stand the tension any longer. 'Well?' he said sharply.

Zoe blinked in surprise. 'Well what?'

'Are you or aren't you?'

She looked at him as if she didn't have a clue what he was talking about. 'Am I or am I not what?'

'Pregnant.'

There was a pause, and then an astonished, 'What?'

'You heard. Are you pregnant or not? Don't look so shocked,' he added coolly. 'I saw the box.'

'When?'

'Two weeks ago. The night before I left for the States.'

'And you've waited all this time before saying anything?'

'Yes.'

'Why?'

'I thought you'd tell me in time. But you didn't.'

'Why didn't you just ask when you found it?'

Bloody good question, and one he couldn't—didn't want to, perhaps—answer. 'I'm asking now.'

'Well, don't worry, I'm not pregnant,' she said with a dismissive wave of her hand. 'There's no baby.'

Another woman, another time, but exactly the same words said in exactly the same way and something inside him went very cold. 'There's isn't now or there never was?'

'There never was.'

'Are you sure?'

'Of course I'm sure. I was late. I thought it wise to do a test. But the day you left for the States I got my period.'

'Thank God.' The relief was staggering, although whether it was relief that she wasn't pregnant or relief that she hadn't been lying to him he didn't know.

Zoe frowned. 'What's this all about, Dan?'

'I'm sorry. I thought…' He shook his head then pushed

a hand through his hair and gave a tight humourless laugh. 'Well, you don't want to know what I thought.'

'Actually,' she said, folding her arms across her chest and looking at him so steadily that he knew she wasn't going to let him get away without explaining, 'I do.'

As the clock ticked loudly in the ensuing silence Dan sat brooding and unresponsive for such a long time that Zoe was beginning to think he wasn't going to tell her what he'd been thinking or what was going on. By now, though, she was desperate to know because the conversation had taken an unexpected twist and she wasn't sure how she'd respond if he shrugged and told her it was 'nothing'.

But then he nodded as if internally agreeing to something and said, 'A while ago I went out with someone.'

'Jasmine?'

'Before that,' he said, his voice eerily flat. 'Way before that. Eight years ago when I was in my mid-twenties.'

'What happened?'

'She got pregnant.'

As there wasn't any sign of a small child running around, Zoe braced herself. 'And?'

'She had an abortion.'

'Oh.' She didn't really know what else to say to that. 'Why?'

'A baby didn't fit in with her career plan.'

The bitterness in his voice told her he hadn't agreed, but Zoe didn't feel she was either qualified or had the right to judge his ex-girlfriend's actions. 'It happens,' she said.

'I know.' He paused, frowned, and when he looked up at her his eyes were so expressionless, so empty, that her chest ached. 'But you'd think she might have bothered to discuss it with me first.'

'Didn't she?'

'No,' he said bleakly. 'She found out the day after she

got a major breakthrough modelling contract she'd been
after for ages. I was away on business for a few days, and
she didn't bother to wait until I got back because as far as
she was concerned there wasn't any discussion to be had.'

'Oh.'

OK, so she didn't know the full story and maybe, just
maybe, she was a bit biased in Dan's favour, but surely
that wasn't right. Surely if they'd been together at the time,
it was a decision that both of them should have been involved in.

'Did you want it?' she asked.

'Funnily enough, I did.'

Then it had hurt him deeply, and she found she was
hurting for him. 'But what's that got to do with me?' she
asked, a bit bemused about why any of this mattered now.
'And what's it got to do with the offish way you've been
recently?'

He shrugged. 'I don't really know.'

All of a sudden, he looked confused and troubled, his
eyes filling with uncertainty and doubt. And something
else...

Frowning slightly, Zoe leaned forwards and looked a
little closer. What *was* that? Regret? Shame? *Guilt*?

'Wait a moment,' she said, her brain sifting through all
the disparate strands whipping through it and tying them
into a vague kind of plait. 'Have the last two weeks been
some kind of test?'

His gaze snapped to hers. 'Of course not.'

'They have, haven't they?' she breathed, not entirely
sure what to do with the knowledge.

'Don't be absurd.'

'Well, why didn't you just ask me when you found the
box, then?' she asked as the memory of him dodging the
question the first time she asked came back, and all his
weird behaviour she'd mulled over during the last week

slowly slipped into place. 'That's why I've been on the receiving end of all those watchful glances and all those assessing looks, isn't it?' She shook her head in disbelief as
it all became clear. 'You know, I had the feeling you were
waiting for something, and you were, weren't you? You
were waiting for me to show what you perceive to be my
true colours.'

Dan's jaw tightened. 'What does that even mean?'

'You've been judging me against standards set by your
ex, someone you knew *eight years ago*. Why? What the
hell is going on, Dan?'

'I don't know what you're talking about.'

'Yes, you do.'

He looked her, his eyes glittering in the soft light of the
kitchen. 'Maybe I want to be able to trust you.'

'You can.'

He frowned. 'Are you sure about that?'

'Absolutely. When have I ever given you cause to doubt
me?'

'You haven't. Not yet.'

'And I won't. And OK so I didn't mention doing a pregnancy test, but why would I when there was nothing to say?'
She looked at him steadily. 'Think about it, Dan. We've
known each other for what, six weeks? Do you really think
it needed a conversation when it was negative anyway?'

'I guess not.'

'If the result had been different then I'd have told you.'

'Would you?'

'Of course I would. Look, you know as well as I do
that I've done nothing to justify your belief that I'll let you
down. At every stage of this whole thing so far I've been
honest and upfront with you, and I don't plan on changing that.'

He sighed. 'I'd like to believe that but I don't know if
I can.'

For a moment Zoe didn't know what to say. 'Did she really screw you up that much?'

'She and Jasmine and a handful of others who always seemed to have some kind of agenda. Between them, they destroyed my faith in women, yes,' he said flatly.

'So you thought you'd put me to the test?' she asked, still finding it hard to reconcile the warm attentive man she thought she'd got to know over the last few weeks with this cold, suspicious and obstinate version.

'No. Of course not. You're being ridiculous.'

'*I'm* being ridiculous?' she said, now feeling her anger beginning to fire at his constant denial of what she was beginning to think was transparently plain to see. 'I'm not the one who's letting eight-year-old hang-ups influence their life.'

'No,' he said, suddenly icy in his defensiveness, 'you're the one who let *fifteen*-year-old hang-ups influence her life.'

'And I dealt with them,' she said. 'So why don't you try dealing with yours? Because I *don't* need to be put on trial.'

'Can you honestly say you haven't been putting me on trial too?'

It was the arched eyebrow that accompanied his words that did it. 'Of course I can, you jerk,' said Zoe, feeling her blood pressure hit the roof as she scraped her chair back and stood up. 'If you wanted to have complete faith in me you could, because it's there. So as much as you proclaim otherwise I don't think it's a case of not being able to trust women, I think it's more that you just can't bring yourself to. And ultimately it's just safer not to try, isn't it?'

Dan's eyes narrowed. 'Are you calling me a coward?'

'Damn right I am.'

And with that she left.

CHAPTER TEN

WHAT THE HELL did Zoe know about anything? thought Dan grimly, standing in the kitchen and listening to the slam of the front door echoing around the house. She didn't know what it was like to have the heart ripped from you. To have the choice of parenthood removed without even a discussion. To feel so utterly betrayed by someone you thought you loved.

And as for all that crap about putting her to the test... She *was* being ridiculous because he wasn't into games like that. He'd never seen the point and he didn't need the stress. He couldn't be bothered with games or the people who played them.

So why hadn't he just asked her about the pregnancy test outright, then? Why had he waited for her to tell him?

The questions struck him like a blow and he glared at the floor, unable—no, unwilling—to answer them.

He tried to ignore them, but they hammered away until he had no choice but to address them. So he skirted round a vaguely possible response or two involving rubbish about wanting to give her time, it being her decision to tell him, blah blah blah. Weak answers and wholly wrong ones too.

Feeling the denial disintegrate beneath the pressure of the truth Dan caved. God, he *had* been testing her, hadn't he? Unconsciously perhaps, but nevertheless he *had* been testing her, because he desperately *wanted* to be able to trust her.

So why didn't he? Why couldn't he? *Was* he a coward?

Maybe he was, he thought, narrowing his gaze at the floor, because Zoe was right. She hadn't given him reason to doubt her once in the six or so weeks they'd known each other, and so maybe he ought to take a look at the evidence rather than letting his hang-ups screw up his judgement.

Zoe was very different from the other women he'd dated. She was honest and upfront and direct, and refreshingly straightforward. She didn't play games and she didn't dissemble. She'd said she'd wanted fun and passion, which was precisely what she'd gone for and precisely what she'd stuck with. She hadn't let him down, and wouldn't.

He'd thought a while ago that it had been time to address his wariness and cynicism with regards to women, and it seemed he couldn't put it off any longer. Because what was he going to do? Spend the rest of his life alone just because he couldn't bring himself to trust someone? If anything was ridiculous, *that* was. It would suggest that his past experiences had a grip on him that he couldn't escape. That he was somehow beholden to them and the thought of being beholden to anything made his stomach churn.

He wanted Zoe. For how long he wasn't sure, but if they were going to continue with this then he needed to address this problem he had with trust, and apologise. See if she'd be willing to forgive his idiocy and give him a second chance. Basically he needed to pull himself together, step up a gear and show her he could—and did—trust her.

Dragging his hands through his hair, Dan looked up and his gaze fell on the invitation to his cousin's wedding that had landed on his doormat a month ago. When it had arrived he'd answered it, sorted the logistics, then propped it up on the mantelpiece and pretty much ignored it. Now, though, he was thinking about the 'and Guest' that followed his name.

Generally the idea of taking a date to a family event was about as appealing as swimming through soup. The grief he got from his mother and various random aunts about his perennial bachelorhood made his insides curdle at the best of times, and if he were to ever show up with a date at something they'd all have him up the aisle within seconds.

But maybe that was another hang-up he ought to get over, he thought, because making it his life's mission to avoid the female side of his family was a bit pathetic for a man of thirty-three, surely.

He was the CEO of one of the country's leading advertising agencies, for heaven's sake. He managed people and handled challenges on a daily basis. Deflecting the speculation of female relatives—ignoring them if he had to—was something he should have no problem with.

Besides, he was sick of always going to these things by himself. Sick of being an object of speculation and talk, and the target of unwanted female attention.

So tomorrow he'd ask Zoe to go with him. Because he would ordinarily go alone, introducing her to his family would show her how much he liked and valued her. It would show he trusted her. It would certainly prove he wasn't a coward. She might well say no—probably would, in fact, given his recent idiotic mule-headedness—but he'd just have to work on her, because, unless she genuinely didn't want to go, now he was set on this course of action there'd be no dissuading him.

'So do you think you'll ever see Dan again?' Lily asked Zoe the following morning.

Wasn't that the million-dollar question? thought Zoe despondently as she looked at her sister and shrugged. 'I really don't know.'

After the horrible end to last night it didn't seem likely, but, God, she hoped that whatever she and Dan had it wasn't over. She hadn't slept well. She'd tossed and turned all night, reliving the conversation, silently cursing his unflinching denial and driving herself crazy with all the things she'd said but probably shouldn't have. Who was she to try and tell him what his problems were? She was hardly fault free.

'Well, frankly, why would you even want to?' said Lily with a sniff. 'He might be the most eligible bachelor on the planet and whatever but he sounds like he was a complete arse last night. I mean, fancy doing something like that. To you, of all people. You're the most loyal person I know. He's clearly got baggage you do *not* want to end up with.'

'Probably.' Definitely, more like, and an entire train carriage full of the stuff. 'But he has his reasons.' Not that she'd be divulging any of them, even if she hadn't signed that confidentiality agreement.

Lily snorted. 'Well, he's a man so that's one pretty good reason. Self-centred to the hilt, no doubt, so what can you expect?'

After a brief but turbulent marriage to what she tended to describe as a weak, pathetic, unfaithful louse, Lily didn't have the highest opinion of men. And after last night, neither had Zoe, but nevertheless self-centred wasn't an adjective that sprang to mind when she thought of Dan.

'Actually, I don't think he is,' she said, recalling the zest with which he'd adopted the role of her boyfriend all those weeks ago and all the recent effort he'd been putting into building up her self-esteem.

'Well, it sounds like he could definitely work on his interpersonal skills.'

'His interpersonal skills are fine,' she said.

'You're hardly one to judge,' said Lily archly.

'Hey,' she said, indignation momentarily pulling her out of her despair.

'What? You're the first to admit you can be a bit odd and socially inept at times.'

'I prefer quirky.' Dan had come up with that one night when she'd been explaining her love of numbers and she thought it sounded rather good.

'I'm sure you do. And what about "socially inept"? Do you have a euphemism for that too? Because it seems to me that "socially inept" *is* a euphemism for the messes you sometimes get yourself into.'

'Gee, thanks.'

'You're welcome. But why are you standing up for him when he's behaved so appallingly?'

Zoe sighed. 'I have no idea. But he's not altogether bad. Just a bit misguided.'

'Now that is a euphemism,' said Lily darkly.

Maybe it was. 'Did I tell you he asked me to sign a confidentiality agreement?'

Lily's jaw dropped and her eyes widened. 'No! Really?' Then she frowned. 'God, who the hell does he think he is?'

'Someone in the public eye who's been burned before?'

'*How* long have you been seeing each other?'

'A month or so.'

'And hasn't he got to know you at all in that time?'

'I'd like to think he has,' she said with a faint smile as she recalled all the long lazy conversations they'd had.

'So has he ripped it up?'

'I haven't asked him to.'

Lily looked outraged. 'You shouldn't have to.'

Her sister's outrage was catching and Zoe found herself thinking, yes, why hadn't he suggested they forget about it? 'It's complicated,' she said with a sigh.

'It always is. Well, it sounds like good riddance if you ask me,' said Lily, swivelling round to pick up the phone that had just started to ring. 'You're way better off without him.'

Hmm, maybe she was, thought Zoe, finally deploying the logic and reason that had been strangely absent these last few weeks. It wasn't as if they were madly in love or anything. They'd simply been having a hot affair, and, while the sex was great, frankly if Dan was prepared to suspect the worst of her quite so quickly, did she need him? No, she most certainly did not.

'Think of him as a stepping stone to bigger and better things,' said Lily, before turning her attention to the call.

'You're right. I will.' Eventually. Once she'd got over the disappointment that they were over she'd maybe start online dating again. Surely great sex and a great man couldn't be all that hard to find...

'What?' she asked, dragging herself away from thoughts of great sex to find Lily watching her, an odd expression on her face.

'The stepping stone.'

Despite everything that had happened in the last twelve hours Zoe's heart lurched. 'What about him?'

'He's here.'

Her mouth went dry. 'Here?'

'Downstairs. To see you, apparently.'

'Why?'

'Well, how would I know?'

'Does he know I'm here?'

'Yes, but I could always fob him off and tell him you're in a meeting or something.'

Ignoring the brief temptation to tell her sister to go for it, Zoe reminded herself that she no longer shied away from conflict, and set her jaw. 'No, it's fine,' she said. 'I have a few things I'd like to set him straight on anyway.'

Lily grinned and punched the air. 'Way to go, sis.'

* * *

Quite what sort of reception Dan had been expecting he wasn't sure, but the minute the lift doors opened and Zoe stepped out he could see the one he was getting.

He watched her approach, her stride efficient and purposeful, her expression cool and haughty and her smile neutrally professional and nowhere near her eyes, and he half expected her to hold out her hand for him to shake.

She showed no sign of the kind of disturbed night he'd had. She didn't look as if she'd spent the early hours pacing the width of her bedroom asking herself how she could have been such an idiot to put into jeopardy a fling she'd been enjoying. She looked gorgeous, magnificent and, unsurprisingly, as inscrutable as the Sphinx.

'Dan,' she said coolly, her voice echoing around the lobby and her heels tapping against the marble floor as she came to a stop in front of him.

'Zoe,' he replied, reminding himself why he was here and why he couldn't just haul her into his arms and kiss the daylights out of her.

'I didn't think I'd be seeing you again.'

'I don't blame you.'

'What do you want?'

'Well, now, that's not very polite.'

'I'm not feeling very polite.'

No, well, in all honesty he couldn't blame her for that either. In fact, the blame for everything that had happened in the last week or so lay entirely with him. 'That's fair enough, I suppose.'

'And I'm *extremely* busy this morning,' she added with a pointed glance at her watch.

'Then I won't take up too much of your time.'

She folded her arms across her chest and arched an eyebrow. 'Well?'

'I'd like to apologise for last night,' he said.

'Fine.' She shrugged as if she couldn't care less about his apology and for a horrible moment Dan had the nasty feeling that he'd lost her.

He cleared his throat to get rid of the sudden tightness. 'The whole pregnancy thing freaked me out a little.'

Her eyebrows shot up. 'A little?'

He shoved his hands through his hair. In his imagination this conversation had gone a damn sight better than it was in reality and he'd been far more in control. 'OK, a lot.'

'Are you still freaked out?'

'No. But I am sorry for unleashing my baggage on you like that. It wasn't fair.'

She nodded. 'It wasn't. You wildly overreacted.'

'I did.'

'Look, Dan, I can understand that a pregnancy scare might have brought up a whole host of memories you'd rather forget and I get that you were feeling jet-lagged and vulnerable and spooked and whatever, but, you know, not all women are the same.'

He stifled a wince at the mention of vulnerability and focused on what she was saying about all women not being the same. 'I know.'

'Do you?' She sounded sceptical.

'Well, I'm beginning to learn through you.' Her expression softened a bit and he felt a stab of hope that maybe he hadn't messed it up completely. 'I'm sorry for doubting you,' he said, wondering if she could possibly be aware that he'd apologised more in the last ten minutes than he had in his entire adult life.

'If I had your issues I'd be asking you to prove it.'

'I'm glad you don't.'

She frowned and alarm began to trickle through him. 'I don't like these games, Dan.'

'There'll be no more.'

'Are you sure?'

He nodded, once. 'I'm sure.'

Zoe didn't say anything to that, just regarded him so thoughtfully and so lengthily, winding the tension so tightly within him that Dan couldn't stand it any longer. He shoved his hands in his pockets, fixed his face so it didn't look like he cared too much about her answer and asked, 'So are we OK?'

Well, really, what could she say in response to such a swift and heartfelt apology but yes? thought Zoe, the last grain of her crumbling resolve to be all cold and steely disintegrating.

She'd never been one to bear a grudge—on the rare occasions she and her sister had come to varbal blows, she'd found a hug and an apology went a long way to clearing the air—and for someone who in all likelihood wasn't used to doing it, Dan's had been so sincere and so unexpected that her resistance had begun to crumble the minute he'd issued it.

Oh, who was she kidding? Her resistance had begun to crumble the second she'd stepped out of lift and seen him standing there, somehow looking rumpled and disorientated and way less sure of himself than usual. She'd seen the dark circles beneath his eyes, the stubble on his jaw and caught the uncertainty written all over his face and, despite agreeing with Lily that she was better off without him, her heart had begun to melt while her brain had threatened to capsize.

And she might have just about stopped herself throwing herself into his arms by focusing on staying frosty and aloof and reminding herself that he was in the wrong here, and that she wasn't giving in any more, but the moral high ground was a lonely place to be and it was so good to see him when she hadn't been sure she ever would again.

'We're OK.'

Dan blew out a breath and grinned, his face transformed into looking a lot brighter than he had five minutes ago. 'Thank God for that.' He yanked his hands out of his pockets and shoved them through his hair. 'I'm so sorry for being such an idiot.'

'That's OK. And you don't have to keep apologising.'

'I'm sort of getting used to it.'

Zoe found herself smiling too. 'You can stop.'

'Fine. But you were right about one other thing too.'

'What other thing?'

'I think maybe I *have* been a bit of a coward.'

'Ah, about that...' she said, her smile fading as she briefly winced. 'Now I have a feeling it's my turn to apologise. I'm sorry, I shouldn't have said it. I was out of order.'

Dan waved a hand. 'Don't be. I don't think you were. And I think I needed to hear it.'

'Really? I mean, I'm hardly one to be lecturing about failings.'

'Doesn't matter. You did and it's fine because I now have plans to change that.'

Zoe looked at him quizzically. 'How?'

'There's something I'd like to ask you.'

For some reason her heart began to thud. 'Fire away.'

'I have a wedding a week on Saturday.'

'That's nice.'

'And I was wondering, would you like to come?'

As the invitation sank in the first thing to hit her was disappointment, although why she should be disappointed she had no idea. The second thing was surprise because by inviting her to a wedding where presumably he'd be introducing her to friends he was showing her he was ready to take what they were doing to a whole new level. The third thing that she felt was a delicious warmth precisely *because* he seemed to want to take what they were doing to a whole new level.

And then she panicked.

She didn't like weddings. Or any social occasion much for that matter, but weddings especially because there were always so many people and so much small talk and so much potential to screw up. If social occasions were like crossing the Atlantic in a dinghy weddings were minefields, and this one would be no different, even with the reassuring presence of Dan at her side.

'A wedding,' she said, trying not to let the panic show in her voice.

'Yes. Next Saturday. If you're free.'

She was as it happened, but it would be so easy to say she wasn't. To say thanks but no thanks, and spend the whole of next Saturday holed up at home with her phone switched off.

For a moment she was tempted to do exactly that, but only for a moment because for one thing it would be an outright lie, and, quite apart from not wanting a repeat of the mess that had ensued the last time she'd tried it, lying outright didn't sit well with her. For another, with Dan standing so close and watching her so intently she'd never be able to do it convincingly. He'd see through her in a second, and then she'd be in an even worse position.

But how *was* she going to get out of it? she wondered and racked her brains for a suitable excuse.

'Isn't it a bit late to let them know?' she said, hoping that perhaps this aspect of wedding planning might have escaped him.

'It's a family wedding—it'll be fine.'

'A family wedding?' Was that worse or better?

'On my mother's side. My second cousin. He's marrying an actress.'

'Big or small?'

A flicker of amusement momentarily eased the serious expression on his face. 'The bride or the wedding?'

'The wedding,' she said, thinking that this was *not* the time for humour.

'Huge. Unfortunately. He's an earl and there's a *lot* of family.'

Yup. Worse than her worst nightmare. 'I don't know...' she said, shifting her gaze to the revolving door, which was beginning to spin with a couple of people making their way in. 'Would it really be all that appropriate to take a fling to a family wedding?'

At the ensuing silence Zoe looked back at him and thought she saw him pale a little. His jaw tightened and his smile faded and any hint of amusement had vanished. 'Forget it,' he said flatly. 'I shouldn't have asked.'

And then it struck her that what with the edginess and the abruptness and everything this was a big deal for him. Well, of course it was. He was asking her to a family wedding, and presumably, if it was so close as to take place a week on Saturday, he hadn't originally intended to ask anyone.

For a man who didn't do long-term and shuddered at the idea of commitment, it *was* a big deal. And so maybe she shouldn't be resisting it quite so stubbornly, at least not without some kind of explanation.

'You're probably busy anyway,' he drawled as if it didn't matter one way or another, and Zoe dragged her attention back to him.

'No, wait,' she said, giving her head a quick shake and pulling herself together. 'Let me explain.'

'You don't have to explain anything,' he said, his expression utterly inscrutable. 'I just thought the afternoon would be more fun if you were there, but if you don't want to go with me that's fine.'

'It's not that.'

'Then what is it?'

God, where to start? 'I'm just not very good in social situations.'

Dan frowned. 'I hadn't noticed that.'

'No, well, that's because you haven't seen me in very many. But generally I'm rubbish. I don't do well at parties and things. Great crowds of people make me panic so I tend to lurk in the background and run if anyone so much as looks in my direction. And I never ever say the right thing. Why do you think I spend so much of my time at work?'

He regarded her thoughtfully for a second then said, 'This is the self-esteem thing again, isn't it?'

'Very probably.' But who cared why? The fact was that if she went, apart from it completely stressing her out, he could well end up regretting asking her and even maybe ruing hooking up with her in the first place. 'Look, what I'm trying to say is that if I went to this wedding with you I'd either be skulking round the edges of the marquee trying not to be noticed or I'd say something idiotic. Either way I'd ruin it for you.'

'Given that my mother will be there it'll be pretty much ruined anyway.'

'What do you mean?'

'Whenever there's a wedding in the family there are bets on how long it'll be before I'm the one heading up the aisle.'

'And you're not planning to do that any time soon?'

'Certainly not.'

Zoe ignored the dart of whatever it was that shot through her at that. 'Then why don't you just not go?'

'I'm the best man.'

'Oh. Well, yes, I can see how that might require your presence,' she said with a nod. 'But don't you think that turning up with me might fuel the speculation and make things worse?' Not to mention the fact that presumably he'd be otherwise engaged a lot of the time so she wouldn't even have his reassurance to keep her on the straight and narrow.

'Undoubtedly, but I've discovered I don't particularly care any more. Let them speculate.'

'You've given this a lot of thought.'

He shrugged. 'Some. It had also occurred to me that your presence would have helped fend off the chief bridesmaid, but I dare say I can manage on my own.'

That grabbed her attention. Who the hell was the chief bridesmaid? 'The chief bridesmaid?' she said, feeling her eyes narrow.

'She came up to me at the engagement party and told me how much she was looking forward to me fulfilling *all* of my best-man duties. Then she kissed my cheek, muttered something about there being copious amounts of mistletoe on order and gave me a wink that I can only describe as lascivious.'

The strength of the jealousy that scythed through her took her so by surprise that Zoe scowled. 'That's *such* a cliché.'

'I don't think she particularly minded about that.'

'Did you?'

His eyes darkened and his expression turned serious. 'I'm not interested in her. Or anyone for that matter at the moment, apart from you. But like I said, if you really can't stand the thought of coming with me then I'm sure I'll be able to manage.'

Zoe bit her lip. Maybe she was slightly overreacting about this. Maybe she was being a bit too uncooperative, a bit too stubborn. OK, so weddings weren't her favourite way of passing the time, but it wouldn't be the first she'd ever been to. Couldn't she get by, the way she usually got by, by going on body language and making sure she thought before she spoke?

Besides, she was trying to get out of her rut, wasn't she? And hadn't she originally thought that she should watch and learn and maybe pick up a few interpersonal skills from him? She could hardly do that within the four walls of a bedroom, could she?

And if this was what Dan had meant by changing his ways, then perhaps she ought to support him in his endeavours. And if he was making an effort to overcome his issues, then shouldn't she?

'I suppose I could come with you,' she said eventually. 'I mean, with all those celebrities floating around no one's going to be interested in me anyway, are they?'

Some of the tension eased from his body and his mouth curved into the beginnings of a smile. 'Probably not.'

'That chief bridesmaid sounds like she could be rather tenacious.'

Dan grimaced. 'She makes a terrier look like a poodle.'

'And if anyone asks I could always tell them I'm just using you for sex, I suppose.'

'That would certainly liven up the proceedings.'

Zoe grinned and, checking that no one could see, reached up to give him a quick kiss. 'Then I guess I'd better dust off my hat.'

CHAPTER ELEVEN

THIS MIGHT VERY well be the wedding of the century, thought Zoe, sliding into a pew halfway back on the right and clutching the order of service as she gazed around at all the beautiful people beginning to fill the church. She wasn't really all that much into celebrity gossip, but already she'd spotted two TV personalities and a supermodel, and given that there were four hundred people at this wedding and the high-profile nature of the Oscar-winning bride and the aristocratic groom, presumably there were dozens more she didn't have a hope of recognising.

Darkness was already falling outside despite it being only mid-afternoon and hundreds of candles flickered around the cavernous space, casting warmth and shadows everywhere. A huge tastefully decorated Christmas tree stood in the entrance, holly trailed from the window sills, arrangements of spiced oranges sat on every available surface giving off a scent that reminded Zoe of mulled wine.

She sat down and tried to make herself comfortable on the hard oak bench. Talk about diving straight in at the deep end. Here she was at probably the biggest, most spectacular event she'd ever attended and not only did she not know a soul apart from Dan, she was all by herself. As the stag night had been last night he'd driven to Somerset yesterday lunchtime—with some reluctance as he hadn't wanted to leave her to come alone—while she, having insisted she'd be fine, had hopped on a train first thing this morning, and he'd been so wrapped up in best-man duties that she hadn't seen him yet.

Logically she ought to be terrified. She ought to be sweating and panicking, swallowing back a bundle of nerves and scouring the place for the nearest exit. But oddly enough she wasn't.

Perhaps the wobble she'd had last night over supper with her sister had covered it, she reflected, absent-mindedly flicking through the order of service. Lily had been Googling the impending wedding and devouring the gossip surrounding it, and as the enormity of what she'd taken on had sunk in Zoe had begun to hyperventilate. But her sister, who'd clearly been expecting something of the sort, had calmly thrust a paper bag into her hand followed by an enormous glass of wine and talked her down from the ledge. She'd then stayed the night, stuck to her like glue all the way to the station and had practically got on board the train with her.

Perhaps the lack of nerves was down to the fact that Dan seemed to think she could handle it. Or perhaps she was feeling largely all right because she'd been right in her assumption that no one would be interested in her. None of the millions of air-kisses flying around were aimed at her, no one tried to engage her in conversation, and there were none of the speculative sidelong glances that she'd half-anticipated.

Whatever it was, she was feeling surprisingly at ease and actually glad that she hadn't chickened out, so maybe her self-esteem was on the up after all.

While her head swam slightly at this heady thought something flickered in her peripheral vision, and as her skin began to prickle and her heart began to thump she looked up and was even gladder she hadn't chickened out because there was Dan. Standing at the top of the aisle with the man she presumed was the groom, looking breath-stealingly handsome and remarkably relaxed for someone who'd previously considered attendance at a family wedding a fate worse than death.

At the sight of him, so tall and upright and gorgeous in a morning coat that emphasised the breadth of his shoulders, her heart lurched and she sighed softly. It had only been forty-eight hours since she'd last seen him but what with the way she was beginning to ache with sheer desire it might as well have been a decade.

His head was bent as he adjusted the cream rose in his buttonhole and she could see him frowning in concentration. Then he went still, and, as if aware of her eyes on him, he turned and looked straight at her. His frown cleared and he gave her a faint smile, and then mouthed a 'hi' at her. On the point of melting into a giant puddle of lust, Zoe mouthed a 'hi' back while she was still capable of rational thought, and nodded when he seemed to be asking if she was OK.

For a moment she wondered whether he was going to come over, and if he did how she'd be able to refrain from hurling herself into his arms and dragging him off into the vestry. But then his gaze flickered to her left and as the groom muttered something in his ear he shook his head and turned away from her and then disappeared from view.

Feeling oddly cheated by the loss of the sight of him, Zoe took a few moments to realise that it wasn't just Dan that had disappeared from view. Everything had, and the only thing filling her vision right now was a bright royal blue.

She blinked a couple of times in case her eyes were playing tricks on her but the blue remained. Then it moved, and she lifted her head to see a slim elegant middle-aged woman standing in front of her and looking down at her with avid curiosity.

Zoe's first thought was that her dark hair and dark eyes were so familiar the woman could only be Dan's mother.

Her second, more depressing thought was that if only she hadn't been so wound up by the idea of a wedding of this magnitude she'd have devoted a substantial amount of mental energy to figuring out how she might handle actually meeting Dan's mother. Which with hindsight would have been an excellent idea because if she had she'd have run through a couple of possible conversations in her head and planned something charming and insightful to say instead being unprepared, off-balance and tongue-tied.

As it was, however, she hadn't done any mental preparation, and now all she had to rely on were her wits, and as the sight of Dan had comprehensively scattered those they weren't all that great a resource.

Swallowing back the knot of nerves that was lodged in her throat, Zoe reminded herself about the progress she was making and the faith Dan seemed to have in her, and got to her feet. 'Hello,' she said and remembered to smile.

'And who might you be?' asked Dan's mother with an imperious arch of her eyebrow and none of the self-doubt that was part of Zoe's make-up.

'Zoe Montgomery.'

'Catherine Forrester.'

She held out her hand and Zoe shook it. 'It's lovely to meet you,' said Zoe politely.

Catherine Forrester tilted her head and regarded her thoughtfully. 'You too,' she murmured, before frowning as if racking her brains for something. And then her expression cleared and her eyes lit up. 'Wait a moment. Zoe Montgomery, did you say?'

'I did.'

'The fake fiancée?'

Under any other circumstances, Zoe might have appreciated Dan's mother's forthrightness. She might even have sensed a kindred spirit. However, in these circumstances all she could do was inwardly cringe, and blush. 'That's right.'

'I see.' Her eyes dropped to Zoe's left hand. 'Still fake?'

'Still fake.' And then thinking she'd better clarify just in case his mother had them walking up the aisle as Dan had suggested she might, she added, 'Not even fake, actually.'

'Then what was my son doing smiling at you like that?'

For a moment Zoe forgot her manners and stared at her. 'Like what?'

'Sort of warmly. Protectively.' Dan's mother tilted her head and considered. 'It was odd. Unusual. When I saw it I had to come over and find out why.'

'Well, I am his date,' said Zoe, telling herself to ignore the heat that flooded through her at the thought that Dan might feel warm and protective of her because he probably felt like that of all the women he dated. 'I've just arrived. I imagine he wanted to make sure I was all right.'

'His date?' said Catherine Forrester, who seemed to have an unerring talent for picking out the details that Zoe least wanted to talk about.

'That's right.'

Her eyes narrowed. 'But I understood you hardly knew each other.'

OK, so this was definitely veering into minefield territory, thought Zoe, reminding herself to think carefully and concentrate. 'Yes, well, we've-ah-kind of got to know each other a bit better since the whole fake engagement fiasco.'

'How well?'

'Well-ish.'

At the thought of just how well she and Dan knew each other, at the very least physically, she felt her blush deepen to a shade that probably clashed horribly with her pale pink outfit.

'I see,' said Dan's mother, clearly and mortifyingly seeing far too much. 'And what are my son's intentions towards you?'

'I don't think he has any.' Unfortunately. Although she was here, wasn't she, meeting his family and friends…?

'Do you have any towards him?'

Slightly disturbed by the idea that she suddenly didn't like the fact that they hadn't discussed the future and deciding that on balance, despite her brave words, she couldn't really tell Dan's mother that she was simply using him for sex, Zoe said instead, 'None at all.'

'Are you certain?'

'Completely.' Although, God, she'd love to have a few. Maybe when she had a chance she ought to ask him where he thought they were heading, if they were heading anywhere at all.

'Hmm, pity,' she said, frowning for a moment before her brow cleared and a gleam of hope flickered in her eyes. 'But you're here. With Dan. And that's a definite improvement.'

'Please don't get your hopes up,' said Zoe, injecting a hint of firmness into her voice as much for her benefit as Dan's mother, 'because I'm really not sure it means anything.'

The gleam flickered more strongly. 'It might mean grandchildren.'

OK, enough, thought Zoe, mentally stiffening her spine. She definitely needed to nip this in the bud because it really wasn't fair to allow his mother to think this might be a possibility when in all likelihood it wasn't. 'Absolutely not.'

The older woman's face fell and she looked so crestfallen that even though she had no reason to Zoe nevertheless felt awful.

But then she rallied and smiled, and Zoe slowly let out the breath she hadn't realised she'd been holding. 'Oh, well, never mind,' Mrs Forrester said airily. 'Perhaps I'll have better luck next time.'

Next time? *Next time*? For some unfathomable reason the thought of Dan with someone else had bile suddenly

rising up inside her but Zoe swallowed it back because of
course there'd be a next time. In the absence of any discussion about the future, she'd always assumed that once they'd
had enough of each other they'd both move on. Didn't mean
she had to like it, though, did it? 'I do hope so,' she said,
just about resisting the urge to grind her teeth.

Catherine Forrester glanced around at the rapidly filling
church and straightened. 'Well, I'd better go and sit down.
It's been delightful to meet you anyway.'

And with that she patted Zoe's hand, and was off.

By the time Dan had managed to shake off Beth, the chief
bridesmaid, with the vague promise of a dance later, and
had tied up a few last-minute best-man duties everyone
had decamped to the marquee for the reception. With the
sheer number of guests it was quite a while before he found
Zoe, but eventually he spotted her on her own studying
the table plan.

When he'd spied her in the church, once he'd recovered
from the oddly intense wave of relief that she was actually there given her original reluctance and the whole mess
he'd made of things before, all he'd been able to see was
the black and pink pillbox hat perched on the side of her
head and the hint of a pale pink outfit.

Now, from behind, he could see that her hair was up in
a chignon thing that his fingers itched to unpin and that
the hint of pale pink was a coat that flared out from her
waist to her knees and made him want to find out what
lay beneath it.

As he walked towards her he saw her straighten and, he
thought, tense a little. When he reached her he put a hand
on her neck, where it met her shoulder, felt her shiver and
heard her breath hitch.

'Hello,' he said softly against her ear.

'Hi.'

'OK?'

She leaned back against him and smiled. 'Much better now. How's the best man?'

'Bearing up.'

'The groom?'

'Besotted.'

'And how was the chief bridesmaid?'

'Limpet-y.'

'Yes, she did seem almost surgically attached to you as you escorted her down the aisle. Rather beautiful, though, in a louche sexy kind of way.'

The hint of jealousy in Zoe's voice made him want to punch the air with something like triumph, which was strange given that displays of jealousy generally brought him out in a rash.

'Perhaps,' he conceded, because whatever else she might be Beth *was* beautiful, and to deny it would only insult Zoe's considerable intelligence. 'But she has a laugh like a hyena and isn't afraid to use it.'

'How unfortunate.'

'It's more than unfortunate. It's been absolute agony. My eardrums are only just recovering.'

In her three-inch heels, Zoe only had to lift herself onto her toes then angle and tilt her head and her mouth was at his ear. 'Want me to kiss you better?'

Dan's pulse spiked. 'That sounds like the best idea I've heard in hours,' he muttered, and unable to stand a moment of not touching her properly any longer he slid his hand down to the small of her back and guided her round the eight-foot high easel upon which sat the giant board.

Out of sight of prying eyes he took her in his arms and lowered his mouth to hers. Zoe wound her arms around his neck and pressed tightly to him as the kiss deepened and heated and threatened to spiral out of control as it always did, and Dan wondered if anyone would notice if they just slipped away and spent the afternoon in bed.

For a moment he was sorely tempted, because however much hot explosive sex they had it never seemed to be enough, but then the laughter and chatter of the guests filtered through the fog in his head and reality intruded and he figured that it might make for an awkward moment if it came to the speeches and he was conspicuous by his absence. So he pulled away reluctantly, his breathing ragged and his body aching with a need that would unfortunately have to wait to be fulfilled.

'God, you smell gorgeous,' Zoe murmured, burying her head in his neck and nuzzling for a moment before drawing back and smiling up at him.

'You look gorgeous.' Even more gorgeous now that her eyes sparkled and her cheeks were flushed. 'Great hat.' He pulled her forwards a little so that he could inspect it more closely and feel her breasts pressing against his chest once more, sucker for punishment that he was. 'And not a speck of dust. I'm impressed.'

'I had to hoover it.'

Dan laughed softly. 'Then it deserves to mingle.'

'I think it might like that.'

Peeling herself off him, she adjusted her coat then dug around in her handbag and took out a mirror and lipstick. Opening the mirror, she checked her hat and her hair and then quickly repaired the damage he'd done to her mouth.

'How do I look?' she asked with a grimace that suggested she wasn't fishing for a compliment but the truth.

Good enough to eat, he thought, balling his hands into fists to stop himself reaching for her and messing up her lipstick again. 'Lovely.'

She dropped the mirror and lipstick back into her bag and snapped it closed. 'Not too badly ravished?'

'Not nearly as ravished as I'd like.'

'Don't worry, there's always later.'

'This is true.'

She smiled. 'I'll look forward to it.'

'So will I.'

Wondering if he ought to be worried at the way she had him wanting to abandon his self-control the minute he looked into her eyes, Dan took her hand and led her into the throng and tried not to think about later because thinking about later would only make walking even trickier than it already was.

'I see you met my mother,' he said, deciding that if ever there was a topic to douse the libido that was it.

'I did.'

'And you survived.'

'Just about.'

'What did you talk about?' he asked, although with hindsight he wasn't at all sure he wanted to know.

'This and that.'

'Sounds ominous.'

'It wasn't. It was fine. She was charming.'

'She can be when she's not trying to tie a noose around my neck. Have some champagne before you meet my sister, as you inevitably will since her curiosity rivals my mother's.'

He plucked two flutes off the tray of a passing waiter and handed her one.

'Thank you,' said Zoe, glancing around as she took a sip. 'You know, Samantha Newark would give her eye-teeth to be here.'

'If she was I'd have her thrown out.'

'Chivalry,' she said. 'I like it.'

So did he, which was another incongruity to add to the collection he seemed to be gathering this afternoon, given he'd spent quite a large chunk of his adult life avoiding it in case it gave anyone any wrong ideas. 'I'm sorry I wasn't there when you arrived.'

'That's OK. It's turning out to be a lot less stressful than I'd imagined.'

'Good.'

'You must have been working hard,' she said. 'The groom looked more relaxed than a groom should.'

'That was probably down to the sedative I slipped into his coffee at breakfast.'

'Really?'

'No, of course not,' he said with a shrug. 'Oliver just knew he was marrying the right person.'

Zoe looked at him over the rim of her glass. 'Have you always been anti-marriage?'

He raised his eyebrows. 'What makes you think I'm anti-marriage?'

'Oh, I don't know,' she said dryly. 'Could it be the weary cynicism in your voice? Or was it that shudder that ran through you when I told the girls we'd been going out for a whole six months back in that bar?'

'You caught that?'

'Impossible not to. I kind of assumed that the shudder at a six-month commitment would extend to marriage. And I imagine your parents' relationship didn't exactly set the best example.'

'Well, no, not particularly,' he said, although he wasn't sure that here and now was quite the right place and time for an in-depth discussion about his attitude towards marriage and commitment.

'What *is* your longest relationship?' she asked.

'A year,' he muttered.

'That's pretty good.'

Good? Hah. 'It was diabolical.'

'Mine's three months. Was yours the one with the traitorous ex?'

Dan felt his jaw clench as the memory of it surged through him. 'That's the one.'

'Did you love her?'

'I thought I did,' he said, ruthlessly stamping it down because he was well over it now, 'but, well, you know what happened there.'

Zoe took a sip of champagne and sniffed. '*I* would never hurt you like that,' she said fiercely.

'How can you be so sure?'

'Well, for one thing I've learned the benefit of putting things out there and talking things through instead of bottling everything up and thinking it'll work out in the end. Because it never does, and a lot of hurt feelings not to mention hideously awful misunderstandings can be avoided with a simple conversation.'

Dan grinned. 'What else, oh, wise one?'

Zoe shrugged. 'Oh, well, I don't really know. I guess that's it for the moment. I'm still learning.'

'So idealistic.'

Her smile faded and her eyebrows rose. 'Don't patronise me.'

'I'm not. I genuinely wish I had your faith.'

She frowned. 'Hmm. Yes, well, I can see why you'd be put off relationships for life.'

'I'm not.'

Dan hadn't meant to say that, the words just sort of slipped out, but now they had, maybe they were true. He was in a relationship with Zoe and, OK, so it hadn't been going on for all that long, but by and large the press had left them alone and things so far had been ticking along quite nicely. So all in all far from being put off relationships he rather thought he actually might be in favour of the things.

Her brow cleared and a light appeared in her eyes. 'It hasn't?'

'No.'

Zoe nodded, as if to herself. 'OK, well, in that case maybe I ought to practise what I preach.'

'What?'

She took a deep breath and something about the way she pulled her shoulders back and lifted her chin had his senses on high alert. 'What are we doing here, Dan?' she said. 'And I don't mean here at this wedding. I mean—'

But whatever Zoe did mean Dan didn't catch because from somewhere he heard a throaty laugh and his head filled with a whooshing kind of noise that blocked out pretty much everything.

And then his brain cleared, and as trepidation began to flow through his veins he turned to locate the source of the laugh and when he found it, when he saw *her*, all the warmth and light that Zoe aroused in him fled, and as memories slammed into his head his blood turned to ice and his stomach turned to lead.

CHAPTER TWELVE

BUGGER.

The question about where they were heading that Zoe had plucked up so much courage to ask had fallen on deaf ears, because while a second ago Dan's focus had been totally on her, now it was most definitely not.

Now, instead of looking deep into her eyes as if they were the only two people in the marquee and enveloping her with a warmth that not even the chilly December air could pierce, he was staring at a point in the distance, his face utterly expressionless and his eyes more shuttered than she'd ever seen them. It was as if he'd sort of switched himself off and the sudden startling change in him was bewildering to say the least.

'Dan?' she said, wondering whether she ought to be a bit worried at the ashen pallor of his face and the tension suddenly gripping his body.

He didn't answer and she got the impression that he was barely aware she was there. He looked as if he were somewhere else entirely, and she would have found the whole thing rather unflattering if she hadn't been so concerned.

'Dan?' she said again, only this time a bit louder.

He whipped his gaze back to her and as he looked down at her, his eyes completely blank, she shivered with a weird sense of apprehension.

'What?' he said, so abruptly, so coldly that she took a quick step back in shock.

'Are you all right?'

'Of course I am,' he snapped, clearly not all right at all. 'Why wouldn't I be?'

'Because you're all tense and you've gone very pale. You look like you've seen a ghost.'

He shot her a humourless smile. 'Merely an ex-girl-friend.'

'Oh?' said Zoe, trying and, she suspected, failing to keep the suddenly rampant curiosity out of her voice. And then because of the strength of his reaction it didn't take her long to land on the heart-sinking conclusion that this wasn't just any old girlfriend. It was The Ex-Girlfriend, the deceitful ambitious cow he'd loved, who'd selfishly put her career first without even discussing it, and torn him to pieces. Nothing 'mere' about that at all. 'Where?'

'By the ice sculpture.'

'It's a vodka luge.'

He frowned at her. 'What?'

'It's a vodka luge not an ice sculpture.'

'Does it matter?'

'It does if I'm going to have to drown my sorrows.'

Which she might well end up doing because she'd thought all she'd have to contend with was an overenthu-siastic chief bridesmaid, but now it looked as if Beth—as she'd discovered she was called—was the least of her wor-ries. Ugh. As she'd suspected when Dan had first issued the invitation this was turning into the wedding from hell, although not for any of the reasons she'd anticipated.

Bracing herself, Zoe scanned the guests near the vodka luge for a likely candidate. 'Which one is she?'

'The blonde.'

She followed his line of sight, craned her neck to see

round a particularly tall man and her jaw dropped. 'Natalie Blake?'

Out of the corner of her eye she noticed his jaw tighten. 'Yes.'

'*She's* your ex?'

'Do you have to go on about it?'

'Crikey,' said Zoe faintly, not entirely sure whether to be impressed or devastated but suspecting she was probably both.

Natalie Blake was a world-famous supermodel whose face and body were on display pretty much everywhere you looked and every time you switched on the television. She was one of the few celebrities Zoe had actually recognised this afternoon, and not just because the picture of her wantonly lying back on that billboard had inspired Zoe's unforgivable descent into statistical inaccuracy relating to lingerie.

In the flesh she was also absolutely stunning, thought Zoe, watching as the woman who famously didn't get out of bed for less than half a million dollars threw her head back and laughed at something while her thick blonde hair rippled down her back.

The knowledge that Dan had once been out with a stunning leggy supermodel, though, was kind of confidence crushing because how on earth would *she* ever be able to compete with such perfection? While there was nothing really wrong with her body she didn't have the pneumatic curves and killer legs that were Natalie's trademark, nor did she have any of her grace.

On the other hand, she thought, her self-confidence perking up a bit, neither did she have Natalie's ice-cold heart. As she'd told Dan s*he'd* never ruthlessly get rid of a baby without discussing it with the father.

So she could be mature about this, couldn't she? After

all, an ex was just that. An ex. And she had to take some sort of strength from that.

Since Dan seemed frozen to the spot Zoe inched closer and asked, 'Do you want to say hello?'

'Not particularly.'

'Well, I think you might have to,' she said, watching the sleek blonde spy them, smile broadly and make her way towards them. 'Unless you want to go and take a turn round the gardens or something,' she added, putting herself in Dan's shoes and thinking that if it were she who'd come face to face with any of her exes, she'd want to run a mile.

'No, it's fine,' he said tightly.

'Would you like me to leave you to it?'

'Don't you bloody dare,' he muttered, slinging an arm around her shoulder and giving her a swift hard kiss right there in the middle of the marquee that rooted her so firmly to the spot that she couldn't have gone anywhere even if she'd wanted to.

By the time Zoe had collected herself, Natalie was in front of them, blinding her with such a dazzling smile and practically drowning her in such charisma that she could see why the woman was signed for multimillion-dollar contracts.

Resisting the weird urge to step between them and fling her arms out to shield him or something, Zoe reminded herself to stay cool because this wasn't about her.

'Dan,' said Natalie, with a throaty kind of purr that completed the whole seductive package and made Zoe's spirits nosedive.

'Natalie,' said Dan with such little emotion and looking so unmoved that she shivered in a way that had nothing to do with winter.

'It's been a long time.'

'It has,' he said. 'This is Zoe Montgomery.' He dropped

his arm from her shoulders to her waist and pulled her in close and it gave her confidence a much-needed boost.

'Oh, the ex-fiancée?' Natalie smiled.

'Long story. Pleased to meet you,' said Zoe, holding out her hand.

'Natalie Blake, and likewise,' said Natalie, shaking it before turning back to Dan with that brilliant smile. 'So how have you been?'

'Fine,' he said. 'You?'

'Great.'

'What are you doing here?' he asked.

'I'm a friend of Helena's.'

'I didn't know that.'

'No, well, we worked together on a film recently and got on.'

'Oh, really,' asked Zoe. 'Which one?'

She named a film that had been a box office number one hit and Zoe wished she hadn't asked.

'You've done well,' said Dan with a smile that didn't wholly reach his eyes.

'I've been lucky. I hear you've done well too.'

'I've worked hard.'

And then they lapsed into a tense little silence that even with all her years of people watching and body language learning Zoe didn't have a clue how to fill. Nor, it seemed did anyone else.

'Well, this is awkward,' said Natalie, her laugh now a bit shaky. 'Look, I'm sorry, I should never have come over. I just wanted to see how you were, Dan. You know, after everything.'

Dan arched an eyebrow. 'Nat, it's been eight years.'

'I know, but I have thought about you. About…well, you know…what happened…'

He shrugged. 'Forget it.'

'I'm sorry I…ah…went about things the way I did…'

'Don't worry about it. It's all water under the bridge.'

'Really?'

'Really.'

'Good.' Natalie let out a sigh of what sounded like relief and smiled. 'Well, it's lovely to have met you,' she said to Zoe. 'I guess I'd better get back to my friends.'

And then she swept off.

Well, that blast from the past hadn't actually been as unpleasant as he'd envisaged, thought Dan, watching Natalie rejoin the group she'd left to come and say hello and feeling faintly bemused by his surprisingly indifferent reaction to her.

Seeing her after all this time had initially been something of a shock, but actually once she'd come over and they'd started talking all he'd really been able to focus on was Zoe. Standing beside him. Pressing against him. Bristling on his behalf.

And it was kind of reassuring, heart-warming, nice. More than nice actually...

'So that was the woman who broke your heart,' Zoe murmured, pressing closer and bristling marginally less than she had been five minutes ago.

'I wouldn't go so far as to say that,' he said evenly, suddenly realising it was true. 'With hindsight I don't think my heart was ever actually involved.'

'She's beautiful, and you know, even though it pains me to admit it, she actually seemed quite nice.'

He narrowed his eyes. 'Hmm.'

'And it looks like she regrets what she did to you.'

'Perhaps.' He might not have loved her as much as he'd always thought but he still wasn't sure he could totally forget the effect what she'd done had had on him.

'Is it really water under the bridge?' she asked, a flicker of doubt and uncertainty leaping in her eyes.

'She certainly is,' he said, thinking that he'd never meant anything more.

Zoe smiled. 'I'm glad.'

So was he. As the Master of Ceremonies called for silence from somewhere on the other side of the marquee he looked down at her, something warm, weird and unidentifiable swimming around inside him. 'Thank you,' he murmured.

'What for?'

'I don't know exactly…Just, thank you.'

'You're welcome,' she said softly, pulling herself out of his arms and giving him a little push. 'You'd better go and get ready to make your speech.'

Zoe heard the groom tap the microphone and begin to speak, but her eyes were on Dan, who was leaning down and saying something to the mother of the bride that made her smile. He was so gorgeous, so confident and so thoughtful. And yes, possibly a bit complicated, sometimes a little rash and occasionally as stubborn as a mule but that only made him all the more fascinating.

He made her happy, she realised with a warm glow. Very happy. He made her wake up every morning they were together with a smile on her face, and she liked it. No wonder she was in love with him, she thought dreamily as her heart melted. No wonder she absolutely adored him.

She watched him for a second longer, smiling and straightening and turning his attention to the groom and then it hit her, properly, and she went still in shock.

Bloody hell. She loved him? How on earth had that happened? And when?

She wasn't even sure she believed in love. To someone generally logical and rational like her, love had always seemed intangible and unquantifiable, and as for the thought of entrusting her well-being and happiness to someone else, well, that had always seemed way too risky to try. She'd told herself that should she ever commit to someone she'd happily settle for sex, friendship and a meeting of minds. She'd never really counted love as a requirement.

But it felt pretty tangible and quantifiable right now, she thought, her pulse suddenly racing and her head filling with a kind of rushing noise. She could feel great buckets of the stuff vibrating through her. It was swelling her heart with amazement and happiness, making it thump crazily against her ribs as if the confines of her chest were too tight.

Dimly aware of the sound of clapping breaking out around her Zoe did the same and raised her glass but hardly noticed that the bride's father had now taken over the microphone.

She was too busy reeling, because the realisation that she was potty about Dan, and probably had been for ages, suddenly made sense of all the feelings that had continually surprised her with their intensity. Such as the hurt she'd felt when they'd had that row about the test he'd subjected her to and the pain when she'd thought that as a result they were over. Or their inconceivability, like the weird way the pregnancy that never was kept creeping into her head, only with the variation that the test had been positive, Dan had been delighted and they'd all lived happily ever after.

And then today, all that lovely warmth that had seeped through her in the church when he'd seen her and they'd had that silent conversation, the jealousy she'd experienced over the prospect of the chief bridesmaid getting her talons into him, the bile that had surged up inside her when Dan's mother had said she hoped to have better luck next time and the despondency she'd felt at the lack of intentions Dan had demonstrated towards her.

And then there'd been that odd protectiveness that had streaked through her when she'd felt Dan tense and seen him pale when he spied Natalie. She'd wanted to plant herself in front of him like a shield or something. Which she'd thought odd at the time, but now seemed perfectly logical because no one messed with the people she cared about.

So had she beaten the odds and found her One? she wondered, her heart pounding and her hands trembling a little with the idea of it. God, she hoped so. She really did.

But was she his One? It was impossible to tell. Yes, he'd invited her here when he'd never planned to take anyone and yes, she got the feeling recently that he might be wanting more, but how much more? Would she ever be able to pluck up the courage and ask? Should she tell him how she felt? Leave it until he did? Agh, these feelings, this situation, the uncertainty and the unpredictability of everything that happened from now on were all so new to her she had no idea what to do.

'Great speeches,' said a voice to her left, yanking her out of the maelstrom of thoughts and emotions that were churning around inside.

In something of a daze Zoe looked round to see a woman beaming at her. Heavens, speeches in the plural? Had she missed all of them? Even Dan's? She really *had* been lost in thought. At least she'd had the benefit of hearing his when he'd practised it on her last week and had had her in stitches. 'Oh. Er. Yes,' she said, managing a weak smile. 'Hilarious.'

'I'm Lizzie,' said the woman, her eyes sparkling and her smile turning even warmer.

'Zoe,' said Zoe, feeling woolly-headed and battered by everything she'd discovered in the last quarter of an hour.

'Nice to meet you,' she said, holding out her hand.

'You too,' said Zoe, shaking it distractedly.

'So, Zoe, you and Dan were looking pretty cosy back there behind the table plan.'

'Were we?' she said dreamily, watching him posing for photographs with the wedding party.

'And Natalie Blake? What's the story there?'

'There isn't one really.' Not any more, she thought, her heart turning over with relief that that obstacle was no longer in the way.

Lizzie grinned and tucked her arm through hers. 'Well, why don't we get a drink and you can tell me anyway? Dan looks as if he's going to be tied up for a bit and I do so love a juicy romance.'

Dan finally managed to pry Zoe away from his sister at around midnight.

'For someone who claims not to like social occasions you certainly seemed to enjoy yourself this evening,' he said, smiling at her as he wrapped an arm round her shoulder and felt her lean on him a little as he led her upstairs.

She laughed softly and clung on all the way down the corridor to their room. 'Yes, well, in all honesty I can't quite see what I've been making such a fuss about all these years, because that was best fun I've had in ages.'

'It was, wasn't it?' He stopped at the door and Zoe bumped into him.

'Sorry,' she said, with an adorably silly smile, her eyes sparkling and her cheeks flushed. 'I think I might have had a bit too much champagne. I'm better with gin.'

'The hard stuff,' he said, unlocking the door and opening it.

She moved past him into the room, her hand brushing against the front of his trousers and she threw him a saucy smile. 'Not yet, but I'll have to see what I can do.'

'Minx.' Dan followed her in, hung the 'do not disturb' sign on the handle and closed the door.

'I know,' she said. 'Who'd have thought?'

She dropped her handbag on the armchair that sat in the corner of the room and then started fumbling awkwardly for the pins that were keeping her hat in place. 'You know, one of the reasons I came to find you the night of your

award ceremony was because I had the feeling you'd un-
leash the real me, and I was right.'

Dan tossed the key onto the console table and glanced up
at her. 'If saucy minx is the real you then I'm all in favour.'

Pausing what she was doing, she shot him a smile. 'Oh,
you are *so* good for me.'

And she was good for him, he thought as he walked
over to her, brushed her hands aside and took over the pin
pulling with the dexterity and efficiency of someone who
was stone cold sober and could actually see what they were
doing. Very good. 'I'm delighted to have been of assistance.'

'Thank you for inviting me.'

'Thank you for coming.'

'I don't think I'll ever forget it. Especially the swans
escaping their pen and invading the dance floor. That was
quite the highlight of the night, I think.'

'*That* was the highlight for you?' he murmured. His
highlights, of which there'd been a few, were far more
mind-blowing, although he had to admit the swans had
been amusing.

'Apart from all the lovely romance of it all, of course,'
she said, sighing and leaning back against his chest. 'And
meeting your sister. She's great. She invited me to her New
Year's Eve party, which I thought was nice of her.'

'She liked you. So did my mother, as she kept telling me.'

She shivered. 'Oh dear. Will you ever hear the end of it?'

'I doubt it.' And actually he couldn't care less.

'What was the highlight for you?'

Where could he even begin to start? Was it the heady
feeling of being free from Natalie after all these years?
The pride and admiration he felt every time he looked at
Zoe this evening? The warmth that filled him whenever
he was near her? The dawning realisation that perhaps he
more than just liked her?

Not sure he was quite ready to share any of that, he

eventually lifted the hat off her head, dropped it and the pins onto an armchair and then put his hands on her shoulders and slowly turned her round. 'I suspect the highlight of my evening is yet to come,' he said softly as he drew her into his arms.

Her eyes darkened and her breathing hitched in her throat. 'Really?'

'Oh, yes,' he said, his heart thundering and his body hardening. 'Assuming you play your part, that is.'

'And what part would that be?'

'Well, now, let's see…' he began, undoing the buttons of her coat and sliding it off her shoulders. 'How about hot wedding guest about to get the ravishing that was interrupted earlier?'

He draped her coat over the chair and set to work on the zip of her dress.

'I think I could make that work,' she said huskily.

'Why don't you just let me do all the work?' he said, lowering his head and putting his mouth to the spot where her jaw met her ear.

She shivered, just as he'd known she would. 'Oh, all right, then,' she said with a long-suffering-sounding sigh, 'if you insist.'

Dan let her dress fall to the floor and sank to his knees in front of her, and murmured, 'Oh, I absolutely do.'

And as conversation faded and the only sounds in the room became moans and groans and harsh ragged panting and desperate little cries he thought he could feel her touching him a little more possessively and holding him a little more tightly.

By the time she was clutching at his shoulders and convulsing around him and he was buried deep inside her, his heart thundering with everything he felt for her, the only thing he could think was that he wanted to stay there for ever.

Because while the night before he'd left for the States he'd thought he might be falling for her, Dan knew that there was no longer any 'might' about it. Zoe was brave and strong, protective and loyal, faced her problems head on and feared nothing, and he was head over heels in love with her.

He was still reeling from the discovery of it the following morning when he stepped out of the shower, wrapped a towel round his waist and at the knock at the bedroom door headed over to open it. Still a bit stunned by the strength of his feelings for her and the mad combination of happiness and panic that they aroused in him. And still recovering from the blistering hot shower he and Zoe had just shared.

So when he opened the door to collect the breakfast and variety of newspapers he'd ordered and caught sight of the headline, when he turned the pages and saw what she'd done, the devastating sense of betrayal hit him like a punch strong enough to throw him against a wall. It winded him, ripped his heart from his chest and filled him with such awful bone-crushing pain that in defence his body went numb and his brain shut down.

CHAPTER THIRTEEN

ZOE CAUGHT SIGHT of her flushed cheeks and sparkling eyes in the steamed up mirror of the bathroom and couldn't help grinning.

Last night had been amazing. She'd talked her head off, danced willingly for the first time in her life, so high on champagne and love that she hadn't wanted to come down. She still didn't because last night had been one of the best nights of her life and she wanted to cling onto it for as long as possible.

Everyone had been so friendly, so warm and so interested in her. Talking to Lizzie about everything and nothing had been such a blast, and Celia had been lovely and then moving on to dinner, well, she'd managed to negotiate that with none of the dread she usually felt at such things. Conversation had come to her more naturally than it ever had and for the first time in her life she'd felt completely at ease and normal.

And it had all been down to Dan and the wonderful effect he'd had on her. He'd helped her release her full potential. He'd uncovered the real her and given her the courage to locate and build up her self-esteem. He'd turned her into the person she'd always wondered if she could be and she'd be for ever grateful to him for that.

She liked to think that she'd had as positive an effect on him as he'd had on her too. He certainly seemed a whole lot more relaxed now than he had been when they'd first met, she thought, turning away from the mirror to pull on one of the complimentary dressing gowns hanging on the back of the door and slip into it. He laughed more, talked more openly and readily.

During the long hot shower they'd just shared, he'd lavished such care and attention on her that she'd felt worshipped. Cherished. Adored. It had been different, and it made her wonder if maybe he felt the same way about her as she did about him.

Zoe felt her heart ache with hope at the possibility that he might. Could she really be so lucky? She, who'd always been so hopeless at relationships…Could it really be her turn?

The more she thought that maybe she could and maybe it was, the more the uncertainty over whether he might love her as much as she loved him began to bug her. She wanted to know. One way or another. Now. She'd chickened out last night when he'd asked if the rampant swans were really the highlight of her evening, but she couldn't hold back any more. She was absolutely nuts about him and she couldn't not let him know how she felt a moment longer.

She heard the bedroom door slam and she jumped into action. With her heart hammering, her body zinging with excitement and her head swimming with visions of the possible future, Zoe tied the belt and flung open the shower-room door.

And at the sight of Dan striding towards her, stopped dead.

As did he.

His face was white, she saw, concern instantly obliterating all thought of asking him how he felt about her. His eyes and his expression were blank and he stood there as still and solid as a rock, but his jaw was tight and his body was vibrating with such tension that she had the impression that all she'd have to do was touch him and he'd shatter.

Behind him the breakfast cart with its shining domes and mouth-watering aromas remained abandoned at the door. The papers lay strewn all across the bed. It felt as if the temperature in the room had plummeted and a sudden feeling of dread swept through her.

'What is it?' she asked, rushing to him and recoiling in shock when he jerked away from her. 'What's happened?'

'This happened,' he said, his voice cold and tight with barely restrained fury as he thrust a paper—one of the tabloids—at her. 'You happened.'

Zoe took the paper, her hands suddenly trembling uncontrollably. With her heart in her throat she looked down at the front page and in a numb daze she read the headline that basically screamed kiss-and-tell. She looked at the photos of her that she'd let be taken and the archive pictures of Dan, and then on legs that were turning to water she stumbled over to the bed and sank down onto the mattress a second before her knees gave way.

Somehow she managed to read the words that started on page one, and somehow she managed to turn to pages four and five where they continued.

And with every word she read she went a little bit colder, her heart beat a little bit slower and her horror increased that little bit more because, oh, God, it was all there. Every single thing she'd told Lizzie—who'd seemed so interested and friendly—in relentless appalling quoted detail. The bullying she'd suffered at school, the names of the girls behind it and what she thought of them. The way she and Dan had met and the circumstances that had led to the 'engagement'. His three-date rule and the confidentiality agreement she'd agreed to sign. His relationship with Natalie—although thank *God* she hadn't mentioned the abortion—and his feelings towards his mother and his aunts.

Oddly she didn't give a toss about the gorily personal stuff about her. She didn't care about how it might affect her reputation or Lily's or that of their business, although that was something she'd have to figure out later. Right now all she could think about were the things she'd revealed about him.

Indiscreet didn't come close to describing the way she'd spilled the information. It was as if Lizzie had slipped her a truth drug and to every question she could now see hadn't been simply the friendly enquiry she'd thought at the time, she'd given an answer. A full, in-depth and sometimes highly personal answer.

She'd done what she'd sworn she'd never do. She'd kissed and told.

As the enormity of what she'd done sank in shame swept through her and a cold sweat broke out all over her skin. 'Dan, I—' she started with no idea of how to continue because she couldn't even begin to work out where to apologise.

'How could you?' he interrupted with such icy calm that she flinched.

'I didn't mean to,' she said, and inwardly cringed because it sounded so lame, so wholly inadequate.

'How could you have been so bloody naïve?'

'I just…well, she seemed nice and interested and asked so many questions and…' She tailed off, unable to look him in the eye, unable to look at him at all, in fact, so great was the shame pouring through her.

'Of course she was interested,' he said, his voice too eerily calm and in control for a man who was clearly beyond furious. 'Of course she asked questions. She's a bloody journalist.'

'But I didn't know that,' said Zoe, beginning to feel a little desperate because this was bad, very bad, and she didn't know what to do. 'She implied that she was a distant cousin.'

'A cousin?' he echoed in chilling disbelief. 'And you believed her?'

'I didn't have any reason not to.' Although she hadn't exactly asked many questions of her own, had she?

'She was there to cover the wedding for one of those celebrity gossip magazines. How could you not have known?'

Zoe let out a little nervous hysterical laugh. 'Well, you know how bad I am with people.'

For a moment there was utter silence. Silence so absolute that Zoe could hear the rustling of the leaves of the tree outside their window. The thumping of her heart. The slow breath that Dan blew out as if to release the pressure that had built up inside him. Silence that went on for so long that Zoe thought he'd accepted her defence. Accepted her apology and was maybe ready to forgive her for her stupidity and move on.

So she risked a glance at him and as her stomach somersaulted she saw that he didn't accept her defence or her apology and whatever they might have had was now hanging in the balance because his eyes were blazing, the pulse at the base of his neck was pounding and his face was thunderous.

'Bad with people?' he said, practically exploding. 'Bad with people? *That's* your excuse for this?'

Zoe leapt to her feet, racking her brains in an effort to work out what she could say to make things better. 'No, of course not,' she said quickly, panic sweeping through her at the realisation that there wasn't anything she could say to make it better. 'There is no excuse.'

'No, there isn't,' he snarled, 'because you *know* the press are interested in me, you know the efforts they'll go to to get even a crumb of information and you handed them everything. On a bloody *plate*.'

The only thing she could do was continue with the genuine regret, take his fury and his accusations on the chin and wait for his anger to blow out. Hope it did. Hope this wasn't the end, that she hadn't screwed things up for good.

'If I'd known she was press,' Zoe said, her throat thickening at the thought that she might have ruined everything, 'I'd have walked away the minute she came over and said hello. You must believe that.'

'Must I? Why? Didn't you stop and think about what you were doing even for a second?'

'No.'

'Why the hell not?'

'I was distracted.' She'd been so dazed and stunned she hadn't been thinking clearly at all.

'By what?' he all but shouted. 'What you were going to get out of it?'

Her jaw dropped and a stab of shock wiped out any idea she might have had of telling him exactly why she'd been so distracted. 'What would I get out of it?'

'I don't know. Money?'

'I have plenty,' she said. 'And I *didn't* do this deliberately.'

He shoved his hands through his hair and narrowed his eyes. 'No, I wouldn't have imagined you would, because you're not stupid and, forgive me if I've got it wrong, but don't we have an agreement?'

Zoe blanched and her mouth went dry. 'What do you mean?'

'The confidentiality agreement you signed. You've breached practically every word of it.'

'What do you plan to do about it?' she said, horror now filling every cell of her body because if he sued, she could lose everything; Lily could lose everything.

'I'll let you know.'

She took a step towards him and felt the panic escalate

when he took one back. 'Look, Dan,' she said desperately. 'I'm sorry I made a mistake. More than you can possibly know. If there's anything I can do to make things better I'll do it. I'll apologise to Natalie. I'll talk to your mother. Your aunts. Whatever it takes.'

Dan just stared at her, a look of stunned incredulity on his face. 'Do you really think I'd want you going around like the loose cannon you are making things worse?'

'Then what can I do?'

'Nothing.'

And then it struck her that she had really screwed up. 'So is this it?' she asked, hardly able to believe that they were over.

'I think so, don't you?' he said flatly.

'You really won't forgive me?'

'I don't know that I can.' Dan shot her a look that was so bleak, so horribly cold and resigned that her heart twisted in pain. 'Oh, what the hell does it matter anyway? I knew you'd let me down in the end.'

Zoe went still. Hang on a minute. Wasn't he even going to try and fight for this? Had she got it so badly wrong? Didn't he feel the same way about her as she did about him? She'd been so sure he did. 'What?'

'You said you wouldn't let me down, but you have.'

'I know. And I'm sorry.'

'What's the point of being sorry when we both know that at some point in the future you'd do it again?'

'Not intentionally.'

'But you would.'

'Well, I can't guarantee that I won't, because I'm only human.' And actually that was a point, wasn't it? 'I'm not perfect, Dan, and nor are you.'

'I know I'm not, but I thought you were.'

Huh? She stared at him in astonishment. Did he really think that? No, he couldn't. Not when she was about as far from perfect as it was possible to be. 'Wait a moment,' she said, as it occurred to her that they might have been here before and she filled with an icy sort of numbness at the thought that it could be happening again. 'You've been waiting for this to happen, haven't you?'

His head snapped up and his gaze locked with hers. 'What?'

'You've been waiting for me to slip up.'

He frowned. 'Why would I do that?'

'I don't know. You tell me.'

'You seem to have all the answers.'

'I don't have *any* answers.' Her brain raced and her heart pounded. 'But now I think about it,' she said as several things struck her at once, 'you know, actually this article isn't all that bad.' She folded her arms across her chest as she looked at him. 'I mean, I didn't say anything that wasn't true, and I didn't mention anything that was really confidential or personal like your business deal in the States and Natalie's abortion. And I know you're upset and you think that I've somehow betrayed you, but it was a genuine mistake, which you'd realise if you weren't being so pig-headed.'

Dan scowled. 'You think this is simply a case of obstinacy?'

'No. I think this is a case of fear. If you're not as anti-relationships as you claim yet you're willing to throw this one away when it's been pretty bloody good then the only conclusion I can draw is that for some reason you're scared.'

He glared at her. 'What would I be scared of?'

'How the hell would I know?' she said, suddenly sick of it all, sick of his irritating air of superiority, his refusal to budge and most of all the way she was practically breaking apart. 'But you've been waiting for me to screw up and, well, congratulations, I have. And you're right. I can't guarantee that it won't happen again, because you know what, unlike you, clearly, I'm not perfect.'

'That much is obvious,' he said darkly.

'Is there anything else or are we done here?' she asked, her throat so achy and tight that her voice cracked.

Dan looked at her with those dark unfathomable eyes of his and Zoe held her breath because after everything they'd been through she couldn't believe that he was really going to let her go like this. Until he nodded and said, 'We're done,' and shattered what was left of her heart.

'Right,' she managed to get out, swallowing hard.

'I'm going to shave,' he said coolly, as if he didn't have a clue he'd just split her heart and her soul wide open. 'When I come back out it would be good if you were gone.'

'Don't worry,' she said, realising the only way she'd be able to cling onto her dignity was by doing the same, and lifting her chin. 'I will be, because I don't need someone who's too scared of what might happen to give us a go. I don't need someone who isn't prepared to deal with whatever stuff he has to deal with. And I don't need you.' She watched him throw her one last glance before heading into the bathroom and, reminding herself to hang on, said, 'Oh, and I hope you have a really *really* lousy Christmas.'

CHAPTER FOURTEEN

ZOE MIGHT HAVE been way off track when she'd accused him of being scared the morning they'd argued, but her hope that he would have a lousy Christmas had proved prophetic because Dan's Christmas was truly horrible.

Following their blistering row, Zoe had been as good as her word and by the time he'd finished shaving there'd been no sign of her other than the faint lingering trace of her scent. Ten minutes later he'd been packed and on his way back to London too, practically drowning beneath the tidal wave of relief that it was all over.

The relief had lasted a couple of hours. At Reading, however, when he found himself wondering if she'd managed to escape the handful of journalists hanging around the hotel and hoping she was all right and thinking he should at least have driven her to the station, it began to fade and turn into something else, and by the time he'd got home it had become something dark and grim and deeply disturbing because he couldn't work out what it was. All he knew was that it was the reason for the now pretty much permanent scowl on his face, the constant grittiness to his eyes and the edgy restlessness gripping his body, and the increasingly appealing temptation to invest in a punch bag.

The ubiquitous festive bonhomie, which was unavoidable and so bloody *cheerful*, only highlighted his filthy temper. His muscles ached with a tension that he couldn't get rid of no matter how much running he did, his chest felt so pressured that he was beginning to wonder whether it might not be a good idea to make an appointment with his doctor, and his jaw was tight with the effort of not grinding his teeth to dust.

Nothing seemed to alleviate any of it. Not work, not alcohol and definitely not spending Christmas with his mother and sister down in Ashwicke.

What with Zoe's article he'd half expected to be disinvited. He'd even rung to apologise and explain and then dis-invite himself, but his mother—who'd been so completely unfazed by the revelation that he couldn't stand her meddling that he suspected it wasn't actually much of a revelation—wouldn't hear of it.

So he'd gone, planning to stay a couple of days at the least, in the hope it might lift him out of his black mood. But the two of them had quizzed him so relentlessly about Zoe and why they were no longer together when apparently they were made for each other that late on Christmas evening he'd eventually snapped. He'd told them to get off his back, then, in full view of their stunned expressions, muttered an apology, leapt in his car and sped back to London.

He'd been back for a week and, with his mind pretty much constantly churning with everything that had happened over the last couple of months, it had been hellish. He wasn't sleeping well and his appetite had all but disappeared and as a result he was grumpy as hell.

Now it was New Year's Eve and he was sitting in his drawing room, nursing a tumbler of whiskey in front of a blazing fire and trying not to wonder why he wasn't going to his sister's party because really there wasn't anything to wonder about. He simply didn't fancy ringing in the New Year with a whole crowd of people he barely knew and there was nothing wrong with that.

He certainly wasn't wondering whether Zoe was there

because he didn't want to see her and he was glad they were over. Ecstatic in fact. He didn't need someone he couldn't trust. Someone who let him down. He'd had enough of all that to last him a lifetime and if that meant he was to spend the rest of his life on his own, then so be it because, despite what his mother and sister might think, there was no way in hell he and Zoe were made for each other.

She'd accused him of being scared, and didn't that just prove exactly how little she knew him because, scared? Him? Hah, thought Dan, knocking back the rest of his whiskey and pouring himself another measure. He wasn't scared of anything and he knew he wasn't because ever since he'd gone off the rails when he and Natalie had split up he'd put into place safeguards and controls to ensure it would never happen again.

Frankly, given his behaviour at the time he'd had no choice. OK, so some of that forty-eight hours was still un-accounted for, but he definitely remembered rocking up at Natalie's house, rip-roaringly drunk, ignoring her threats to call the police if he didn't knock it off, and then taking a swing at the unfortunate police officers who'd been on duty at the time and had tried to restrain him. Somehow she'd managed to dissuade them from arresting him, but it had been a close run thing, and once he'd sobered up the knowledge of just how totally he'd lost control and what could so easily have happened because of it had hit him like a freight train and he'd promised himself that once was more than enough.

So he'd kept a tight control on himself and everything that had the potential to affect him. And, apart from the blip that had been Jasmine Thomas, it had worked beautifully.

Until Zoe had come along and shot it all so completely to pieces that he hadn't known which way was up, let alone been able to formulate a proper strategy to handle her.

That she *had* shot it to pieces wasn't in any doubt, he now acknowledged with a start. She'd dragged him into her life and then comprehensively and systematically stripped him of his control, despite his best efforts to prevent it. From the moment they'd met his behaviour had been uncharacteristic and rash and frighteningly unpredictable. He'd recognised her as trouble and he'd responded, but his responses had been haphazard and reactive and impulsive and with hindsight it was no wonder that every single measure he'd put into place to control the way he reacted to her had failed.

Firstly there'd been the kiss-only condition to his decision to help her out at the reunion. That had hardly worked out well. Then there'd been the three-date-only rule, which he'd discarded with reckless justification and indecent haste. And the confidentiality agreement, which had also been a complete waste of time because he had no intention of doing anything with it and probably never had.

When the physical barriers had let him down he'd tried putting up emotional ones, such as the whole pregnancy trust thing, but those had failed too. And then he'd discovered that she had screwed up and, yes, he'd been devastated at the thought she'd betrayed him, but hadn't there also been a tiny grain of relief in there too?

Dan's fingers tightened on his glass as the truth of it smacked him right between the eyes. God. Zoe was right. He *had* been waiting for her to let him down because he'd known he was in deep and he'd wanted to escape and then be able to pat himself on the back for getting out of something that might cause him the kind of emotional grief he'd suffered at the hands of Natalie.

Not the grief of splitting up necessarily but the loss of control that he might experience as a result of it. Because what if he and Zoe made a go of it, and things didn't work out? He hadn't loved Natalie and look what had happened. He absolutely adored Zoe so if it all went wrong the fallout could be so much worse. He lifted the grass to his mouth, and shuddered. The thought of *that* truly didn't bear contemplation.

Although, come to think of it, thought Dan, suddenly going stock-still mid-gulp and nearly choking, wasn't that what had already happened? He was nuts about her and they'd broken up, so weren't things about as bad as they could get? They were. And was he going off the rails? Was he losing control and getting that criminal record he'd been so close to getting last time? No, he wasn't. He might be feeling all shredded and twisted up inside, but he was here. In agony and, for the first time in his life, utterly lost, but he wasn't assaulting police officers and he wasn't drunk out of his skull. Because he wasn't rash and impulsive and twenty-five, and it wasn't his pride that had been battered. This time it was his heart, and the pain of losing Zoe went too deep.

So what the hell had he done? he asked himself, his heart hammering as the realisation of just how much he loved and wanted her slammed into his head. Zoe was the best thing that had ever happened to him and he'd made her leave. He'd stood there in that hotel room all cold and intractable, wilfully choosing not to believe her, deliberately bottling up how he really felt in favour of a sort of righteous fury that had been deeply unfair, totally idiotic and undeserved.

Had he completely lost his mind?

She hadn't tried to deny what she'd done or make out it was anything other than her fault. She'd taken the blame for it fairly and squarely. She was the bravest woman he knew, and not just then.

She hadn't had to go to the wedding with him, but she had. She'd swallowed back her concerns and turned up alone, knowing no one but him. The wedding, what with the four hundred guests, his mother, Beth and Natalie must have been her ultimate nightmare. But she'd dealt with it.

Zoe had courage, way more courage than he had. She'd

had the courage to work out what she wanted, where she was going wrong, and change.

And what did he do? Let things fester. Lose his temper and sulk. Was he really going to let himself carry on getting away with it? It didn't seem the most attractive proposition.

Wasn't it time to put things right? Tell her how he felt about her and beg her for another chance? And if it was, what was he doing still sitting here when he knew where she was going to be?

Jumping to his feet and scooping up his keys, his wallet and his phone, Dan set his jaw and grabbed his coat because it seemed that Zoe wasn't the only one who'd screwed up.

CHAPTER FIFTEEN

THE REASON SHE'D come to Celia's New Year's Eve party had nothing to do with the hope that she might see Dan, thought Zoe, handing her coat to the cloakroom attendant and stashing the ticket she was given in exchange into her bag. Truly, it didn't. It was simply that Lily was doing her own thing and she hadn't wanted to spend the last night of the year on her own. That was all.

She didn't want to see him anyway. She hadn't been lying when she'd told him that she didn't need him. She didn't. Over the last fortnight she'd realised that he might have been a catalyst in her self-discovery but she'd have got there without him on her own—eventually—because she'd decided things needed to change long before she'd met him.

Nor did she miss him. In fact she'd barely thought about him over the last couple of weeks. She hadn't had time and she certainly hadn't had the inclination. She'd had more than enough work to keep her occupied and so the only time he crossed her mind was when she was accosted by a journalist wanting a follow-up to her kiss-and-tell either on the phone or in person, but she'd got good at barking out a 'no comment' and reminding herself just what a bastard he'd been.

No, she reminded herself, pulling her shoulders back and lifting her head as she walked over to the deep red velvet curtain that hung between the lobby and the nightclub, she didn't miss the stubborn deluded idiot. And she was far better off without him. She was. Or she would be when it stopped hurting. Which it would soon enough because she was over it, and she was over him. And she was here to prove it.

She drew back the curtain and she slipped into the club, the noise hitting her like a rocket blast and making her resolve strengthen and her spirits soar. Tonight marked the beginning of a new year, she told herself firmly. A new start. A new her. And she was going to celebrate in style.

What the hell was Zoe doing?

From the bar of the dimly lit, packed and beat-throbbing nightclub Dan was watching her with astonishment. He wasn't sure what kind of state she'd be in after he'd stupidly banished her from his life, but he hadn't been expecting this. If he'd thought about it at all he'd have imagined her standing to one side, nursing a gimlet as she watched the proceedings while perhaps wondering if it would be rude to leave before the clock struck midnight.

But she wasn't doing any of that. She wasn't on the sidelines, she wasn't watching the proceedings and she certainly wasn't showing any signs of wanting to leave. She was wearing a black halter-neck top and tight-fitting black trousers and dancing with an abandon he'd *never* have expected from her. An abandon he didn't actually think he'd ever even seen before. She had her hands in her hair, her body was moving sensuously to the thudding beat of the music, and, bloody hell, was she *gyrating*?

She looked incredible. Wanton. Liberated. And his heart pounded with admiration, desire, longing, adoration and a whole host of other good things he didn't have time to identify, because now she was boogieing up to a man who'd been eyeing her up and shooting him a flirtatious smile, and Dan found he wasn't liking any of it at all.

She clearly hadn't been pining for him the way he had for her, he thought, his stomach twisting painfully as he fought the urge to grind his teeth. She didn't look haggard and drawn. She looked stunning and ecstatic, as if she was having the time of her life, as if she hadn't given him a moment's thought, as if as far as she was concerned he, *they*, had never happened.

The realisation made his heart shudder to a halt and his throat tighten. God, maybe he was too late. Or maybe she'd didn't love him. Based on how she'd held him and the things she'd whispered in his ear that last night they'd spent together, he'd sort of assumed she did but maybe his assumption—or rather presumption—had been wrong.

The possibility that that might be the case nearly brought him to his knees, but he had to remain upright because he hadn't come here to collapse. He'd come to get her back.

He watched as she pulled the man she'd been flirting with onto the dance floor and went into his arms and a sheet of white-hot jealousy lanced through him.

Right. That was it. He'd had enough. Assuming it wasn't too late and he hadn't been wrong—and he really *had* to cling onto that assumption so that he didn't fall completely apart—it was time to try and put things right.

Dammit, this wasn't working, thought Zoe, sweat pouring off her. She'd danced her heart out but it was no use. Because she'd tried so hard to convince herself that she was over Dan, but she wasn't.

For all her fine words earlier she was, and had been for the last fortnight, utterly miserable. Her heart was breaking and she was aching, and all the boozy happiness around her was only intensifying her misery. She hadn't come here just because she hadn't wanted to spend the last night of the year on her own. She'd come because she'd wanted to see him, and to show him she was fine, that she didn't care that he hadn't wanted her.

But she wasn't fine, and she did care. So very much.

And he wasn't here. And because he wasn't, and because her heart was shattering all over again and she was falling apart inside, she was now dancing with a man who seemed to have the eight tentacles of an octopus and was intent on wrapping every one of them around her.

She'd just about managed to keep him at bay while the music had been energetic and thumping, but now, oh, God, it was segueing into something slow and crooning and her dance partner was moving closer and those arms were getting tighter.

But she couldn't summon up the energy to fight him because she now recognised the song as being the one that she'd mentioned they'd danced to in that imaginary nightclub in Italy and it instantly transported her back to the night this had all started, and she was filling with such deep, aching melancholia she didn't think she could stand it.

Once the song finished that would be it, she told herself wretchedly. She'd tried, and Celia put on a fine party, but she really couldn't stay any longer. The yearning hope that Dan would be here and the crushing disappointment that he wasn't was just about ripping what was left of her self-control to shreds.

So five minutes more and then she'd traipse home and drown her sorrows with the bottle of champagne she had in the fridge waiting for who knew what.

Well, *she* knew, she thought, her heart sinking even lower and her throat aching with the lump that had been there for pretty much the entire fortnight, but really it wasn't all that relevant now, not when—

'Mind if I cut in?'

At the sound of the deep voice behind her, Zoe froze, her head went blank and her heart practically stopped. And then as it hit her that Dan *was* here after all, heat and longing and pure relief started rushing around her.

For a second her dance partner's arms tightened around her in what she could only presume was a display of macho territorial possession or something, but Dan must have been shooting daggers at him because his face went a bit white and then his arms loosened.

'Not at all,' said Wilson or Winston or perhaps Walter. Whatever his name was he clearly had the intelligence to sense this was a battle he wasn't going to win, and melted away.

Which left her standing on the dance floor like a lemon with Dan behind her while all around her couples smooched and swayed and she wondered why he was here.

Slowly she turned, and as she saw him she caught her breath. God, he looked awful. There were dark circles beneath his eyes and hollows beneath his cheekbones. His hair looked as if it hadn't been combed for a week and his jaw hadn't seen a razor for days. His eyes were dark and serious and his expression intense and his focus was entirely on her.

Her heart, pathetically weak organ that it was, turned over at the sight of him, but the image of him standing there in that hotel room telling her that he didn't want to see her again was still fresh in her memory and she just couldn't seem to let it go.

'Have a drink,' he said, handing her a shot glass of something cold and clear. 'You look like you could do with one.'

'So do you.'

'Yes, well, I'm in the process of trying to get over an unexpected and almost Neanderthal-like need to protect what's mine. It's thirsty work.' He lifted his own glass, knocked it back in one and then winced and shook his head. 'God, that's foul.'

'Yours?' Zoe echoed, going a bit giddy despite her resolve to stay strong.

He nodded. 'Yes. Namely, you.'

'I didn't know I *was* yours.'

'Neither did I, but I do now.'

Blinking away the giddiness before she got too carried away and threw herself at him, she sniffed her drink gingerly. 'What is this?'

'Grappa.'

The shock of seeing him again and the revelation that he thought she was his made the grappa seem like an excellent idea so she downed hers and gasped as the alcohol hit the back of her throat. 'Are you responsible for the music too?'

'Well, you are wearing black and it is tight, even though it isn't a ski suit.'

Her heart turned over at the thought that he'd remembered the way they'd met—fictionally, at least. 'I hope you're not expecting the rest of the night to pan out in the same way?'

'You mean with us burning up the sheets? Well, that's rather up to you.' He glanced down at her glass. 'Are you finished? Yes? Good.' Dan took her glass and then shot off to put them on a table before striding back. 'This is our song,' he said, taking her hand. 'We should dance.'

Before she could even think about protesting she was in his arms, the hand planted on her lower back holding her tight against him and then she found she was so where she wanted to be that she couldn't protest even if she'd wanted to.

'How was your Christmas?' he asked, looking down, his eyes burning into hers.

Miserable. 'Lovely. I spent it with my parents and Lily in Shropshire. How was yours?'

'Hideous.'

'Excellent.'

'Want to know why?'

'If you must,' she said with a nonchalance that totally belied the curiosity and the longing whipping through her.

'My family drove me mad.'

'If you're after sympathy you're talking to the wrong person.'

Dan shot her the ghost of a smile and it made her stomach flip. 'I don't want sympathy. Even though I probably don't deserve it I'd like your forgiveness.'

She arched an eyebrow, her voice still amazingly cool given the mess she was inside. 'My forgiveness?'

'Yes. Christmas was bad enough but the last week has been almost unbearable.'

'Why?'

'Realising you were right about the being scared thing has been really quite harrowing.'

She stared up at him, her feet suddenly missing the beat at the thought of what that might mean. 'I was right?'

'Absolutely spot on,' he said, stopping for a second while she untangled her feet from his and then resuming the swaying sort of shuffle they were doing. 'I think I've been terrified ever since you came up to me in that pub and kissed me. You blew my mind and shot my world to pieces. That's never happened to me before.'

'I didn't mean to.'

'I know. But you did, nevertheless, and that was when I began to panic.' He pulled her closer and she had to fight back the temptation to lean in further and snuggle because he was so warm and hard and smelled so gorgeous, and it had been *such* a long time.

'The thing is,' he continued while her body sizzled with every brush against his, 'I'm something of a control freak. When Natalie told me what she'd done and why, I went slightly off the rails. Actually,' he amended, 'not slightly. I careered off them so spectacularly I was lucky not to end up with a criminal record.'

Zoe pulled back a little and stared up at him in astonishment. 'Really?'

'Absolutely. Remind me to tell you about it some time. Anyway, it scared the living daylights out of me so I did everything I could to protect myself from it happening again because I didn't want to feel like that again.'

'No, well, I can see why.'

'Actually I still don't, which was why I behaved like a total jerk after the wedding. I'd just realised that I was in love with you and it scared the hell out of me, which was why I so badly overreacted.'

Her heart lurched and then began to bang crazily against her ribcage. 'You're in love with me?'

'Completely and madly. I thought I could protect myself from you, but what I failed to realise is that with you, I have no protection and I have no defence.'

That was just about the loveliest thing she'd ever heard. 'Do you mind?'

'Not any more.' He looked deep into her eyes and her heart melted. 'You have no idea how sorry I am for the way I behaved.'

'It can't be as sorry as I am for the article,' she said, her throat suddenly tight.

'You haven't had the experience with the press I have,' he said earnestly. 'I should have thought about that.'

'And I should have been more aware,' she said, and took a deep breath. 'But the reason I wasn't thinking straight was because I'd just realised how much I loved you and so that Lizzie woman caught me at a particularly vulnerable moment.'

His face lit up. 'You love me?'

'Completely and madly.'

He buried his face in her hair and muttered, 'Thank God

for that,' and then he was kissing her like a man starved and she was clinging to him and kissing him back just as fiercely.

When they broke for breath she could feel his heart jack-hammering against hers and she held him close. 'God, I wish I could undo what I did,' she said huskily.

'I don't,' he said to her surprise. 'What you did wasn't any worse than what I did when I refused to let you go the night of your reunion. I made you face your demons, and you made me face mine. You're a brave woman, Zoe Montgomery.'

'You're no coward yourself.'

'I know.' Dan shot her a quick grin. 'I ripped up the confidentiality agreement, you'll be pleased to hear. How brave is that?'

'Are you sure?'

'One hundred per cent. I've no doubt that we'll both let each other down repeatedly in the future, and on occasion drive each other nuts, but isn't that all part of a relation-ship? The highs and the lows? The good times and the bad? Wouldn't it be rather dull to just trundle along without any of the soaring happiness and the deep despair along with all the other bits in between?'

Zoe compared the way her life had been before she'd met Dan, and the way it had been after and figured there was no contest. 'I think it would.'

'I'm glad you say that because I've been thinking that our relationship might have briefly started out as a cha-rade, but the irony is that you *are* the east to my west *and* the north to my south.'

'Weren't you the east to *my* west and the north to *my* south?'

He thought about it for a second then grinned. 'Does it matter which direction we're going in as long as it's the same one?'

'Not really,' she conceded and then took a deep breath. 'Are we? Going in the same direction, I mean.'

'I hope to God we are.' He looked deep into her eyes. 'Because I absolutely adore you.'

As he lowered his mouth to hers she slid her arms around his neck and kissed him with everything she felt. She was so deliriously happy, so caught up in the kiss, in him, so barely able to believe that things had turned out this way, that she didn't hear the clock strike twelve. She didn't hear the cheers and the clapping and she was hardly aware of the loud drunken rendition of 'Auld Lang Syne' being sung around them.

It was only when she felt something flutter against her face that she opened her eyes and pulled away.

Looking up and around at the glitter that was floating down from the ceiling, Zoe laughed. 'We've had the song and the grappa, and look, now we have the snow.'

'So we do.'

She kissed him again and then murmured against his lips, 'Happy New Year.'

'I think it will be…' He paused then took a deep breath. 'Especially if you married me.'

Her heart skipped a beat and then began to race. 'Is that a proposal?'

'Yes.'

A surge of brilliant happiness burst through her and Zoe felt her mouth break into a wide delirious smile. 'My second in three months. A record.'

He brushed a silver star off her nose and shivers ran through her as much at the look in his eye as at his touch. 'Well, what would you say to trying it for real this time?'

'I'd say your mother's going to be thrilled.'

* * * * *

Mills & Boon® Hardback

December 2013

ROMANCE

Defiant in the Desert	Sharon Kendrick
Not Just the Boss's Plaything	Caitlin Crews
Rumours on the Red Carpet	Carole Mortimer
The Change in Di Navarra's Plan	Lynn Raye Harris
The Prince She Never Knew	Kate Hewitt
His Ultimate Prize	Maya Blake
More than a Convenient Marriage?	Dani Collins
A Hunger for the Forbidden	Maisey Yates
The Reunion Lie	Lucy King
The Most Expensive Night of Her Life	Amy Andrews
Second Chance with Her Soldier	Barbara Hannay
Snowed in with the Billionaire	Caroline Anderson
Christmas at the Castle	Marion Lennox
Snowflakes and Silver Linings	Cara Colter
Beware of the Boss	Leah Ashton
Too Much of a Good Thing?	Joss Wood
After the Christmas Party...	Janice Lynn
Date with a Surgeon Prince	Meredith Webber

MEDICAL

From Venice with Love	Alison Roberts
Christmas with Her Ex	Fiona McArthur
Her Mistletoe Wish	Lucy Clark
Once Upon a Christmas Night...	Annie Claydon

Mills & Boon® Large Print
December 2013

ROMANCE

The Billionaire's Trophy	Lynne Graham
Prince of Secrets	Lucy Monroe
A Royal Without Rules	Caitlin Crews
A Deal with Di Capua	Cathy Williams
Imprisoned by a Vow	Annie West
Duty at What Cost?	Michelle Conder
The Rings That Bind	Michelle Smart
A Marriage Made in Italy	Rebecca Winters
Miracle in Bellaroo Creek	Barbara Hannay
The Courage To Say Yes	Barbara Wallace
Last-Minute Bridesmaid	Nina Harrington

HISTORICAL

Not Just a Governess	Carole Mortimer
A Lady Dares	Bronwyn Scott
Bought for Revenge	Sarah Mallory
To Sin with a Viking	Michelle Willingham
The Black Sheep's Return	Elizabeth Beacon

MEDICAL

NYC Angels: Making the Surgeon Smile	Lynne Marshall
NYC Angels: An Explosive Reunion	Alison Roberts
The Secret in His Heart	Caroline Anderson
The ER's Newest Dad	Janice Lynn
One Night She Would Never Forget	Amy Andrews
When the Cameras Stop Rolling...	Connie Cox

Mills & Boon® Hardback
January 2014

ROMANCE

The Dimitrakos Proposition	Lynne Graham
His Temporary Mistress	Cathy Williams
A Man Without Mercy	Miranda Lee
The Flaw in His Diamond	Susan Stephens
Forged in the Desert Heat	Maisey Yates
The Tycoon's Delicious Distraction	Maggie Cox
A Deal with Benefits	Susanna Carr
The Most Expensive Lie of All	Michelle Conder
The Dance Off	Ally Blake
Confessions of a Bad Bridesmaid	Jennifer Rae
The Greek's Tiny Miracle	Rebecca Winters
The Man Behind the Mask	Barbara Wallace
English Girl in New York	Scarlet Wilson
The Final Falcon Says I Do	Lucy Gordon
Mr (Not Quite) Perfect	Jessica Hart
After the Party	Jackie Braun
Her Hard to Resist Husband	Tina Beckett
Mr Right All Along	Jennifer Taylor

MEDICAL

The Rebel Doc Who Stole Her Heart	Susan Carlisle
From Duty to Daddy	Sue MacKay
Changed by His Son's Smile	Robin Gianna
Her Miracle Twins	Margaret Barker

Mills & Boon® Large Print
January 2014

ROMANCE

Challenging Dante	Lynne Graham
Captivated by Her Innocence	Kim Lawrence
Lost to the Desert Warrior	Sarah Morgan
His Unexpected Legacy	Chantelle Shaw
Never Say No to a Caffarelli	Melanie Milburne
His Ring Is Not Enough	Maisey Yates
A Reputation to Uphold	Victoria Parker
Bound by a Baby	Kate Hardy
In the Line of Duty	Ami Weaver
Patchwork Family in the Outback	Soraya Lane
The Rebound Guy	Fiona Harper

HISTORICAL

Mistress at Midnight	Sophia James
The Runaway Countess	Amanda McCabe
In the Commodore's Hands	Mary Nichols
Promised to the Crusader	Anne Herries
Beauty and the Baron	Deborah Hale

MEDICAL

Dr Dark and Far-Too Delicious	Carol Marinelli
Secrets of a Career Girl	Carol Marinelli
The Gift of a Child	Sue MacKay
How to Resist a Heartbreaker	Louisa George
A Date with the Ice Princess	Kate Hardy
The Rebel Who Loved Her	Jennifer Taylor

1213 GEN STD LP